ROGUE PLANET

Jeffrey Peter Clarke

ROGUE PLANET

DOUBLE DRAGON

Prologue

Each dawn vanquished stars from the bright morning as always it had. But a day came when one of these stars persisted in the sky. Though at first a merest point of red it soon began to grow, soon to contest the natural light of day. As the planet turned, this new star arose and set as did the parent sun, and with the passing days its angry brightness grew. It crossed the sky with baleful presence, a brazen intruder casting harsh light over land and sea. And though the new star was never to challenge the parent sun's intensity, winds of fearsome strength were born with tides arisen to unprecedented height. The star continued on its way, leaving chaos in its wake. It began to diminish, receding through the span of time in which it had at first appeared, dimming to a merest point until it was altogether gone. Yet its passing had bestowed a fatal legacy, a basic universal force that already was at work.

Time flowed on but with it came ominous change. Through the seasons and through the years the world grew cooler, the parent sun declined by barely perceptible measure, its bounty of heat and light all the while lessening. Passing ages brought ever darkening days, icy seas and freezing air. Eventually, endless nights of frigid stillness ruled though that once benign sun, now distant but still the brightest feature of the heavens, arose and set as if to bid farewell to a world that had once coursed within its domain, a world condemned now to frozen desolation.

Chapter 1 - Planet X

'In an infinite universe there must be infinite possibilities for life. Whatever life forms are possible will somewhere have evolved and must continue to do so.'

I don't recall who made that claim but after my experiences on Mars a few short years ago – Earth years, that is, and just for now I'll stick with those, and more recently on Saturn's largest moon, Titan, I'd believe every word of it. And that's just within our own solar system.

Our journey to Titan on the then advanced DSV, that is Deep Space Vehicle, Orion, had been the first human venture beyond Mars orbit to the outer planets. But here I am once more on Mars, a cold, harsh desert world maybe, but permanent home to tens of thousands of humans, all physiologically adjusted to our gravity which is little more than a third that of the home planet. The majority of them have never set foot on Earth. And if you're not too familiar with the hard facts of life out here then let me remind you how our unbreathable atmosphere is so thin, the air pressure so low, that on most of the surface, water ice will sublimate from its solid state to vapour. That's right, water boils directly from being frozen. Then there's our surface temperature averaging around minus sixty Celsius – plunging as low as minus one-forty at the South Pole in winter with a passing high of almost thirty recorded on rare occasions at the equator.

So maybe you're wondering why people choose to live on what some have described as a glorified rust ball. Well there are a number of reasons for that. It began, of course, with scientific research and a quest to find life, then human visits with bases being set up where sub-surface water was easily accessed and supplies to sustain life shipped over from the home planet. But soon enough people realised they would have to become self-reliant and not exist in caves or the pressurised metal shells of used rockets with little more than a desire to get back to a cosier existence Earth-side. In order to encourage their staying power, Earth shipped out heavy building equipment programmed to do much of the hard work while directed by the would-be residents. The first permanent, as with all later bases, had foundations of basalt, and there's enough of that around. But of prime importance were the biodomes. These were grown organically upwards with that seemingly miracle material, Bioplast. Although modest in size at first, these transparent domes enabled our budding colonists to grow food in a near enough to Earth-like environment and that helped to kill off those crazy ideas some people had dreamt up, before anything sent out from Earth ever landed here, about terraforming the planet. That is, or was, trying to make it into another Earth. But that was many years ago so I can now talk in Martian years, each one being six hundred and eighty seven days; getting on for twice one Earth year. Newcomers joke by expressing their age in Martian years to make themselves sound younger. I seldom think about it since age, old or otherwise, isn't what it used to be. You can't be certain of a person's age by their looks any more.

Okay, this seems a good time to introduce myself: I'm Brett Anderson, ex-military back on Earth but on Mars I'm now Commander Anderson because I've been given, or taken, command of several operations. But what's in a title? Out here you turn your hand to anything that needs it so as titles don't always matter and formalities are not so important, I'm just Brett unless someone feels I ought to be labelled otherwise. Our advances in self-sufficiency began what might be called a scramble with the various powers on Earth, including the United American States, wanting to grab their choice of territory on the red planet so they could mine those elements increasingly rare on Earth and on her moon. Our bases, together with mining and manufacturing facilities proliferated rapidly, in part because Mars, having no oceans, has roughly the same land space as Earth, and because deserts are not as easy to mess up as are forests, fields and seas. The International Space Station was set up in orbit to house emergency supplies, to deal with those rockets from Earth not intended to land on Mars and to handle shuttles whose purpose was to carry their personnel and cargoes to and from the surface. The ISS eventually grew as large as any of those orbiting the home planet and its commander,

Amalia Barbosa, who we'll meet later, eventually became and remains still our official ambassador to Earth.

We've had our disasters; one major event brought about by the interference of outside interests on Earth when a highly advanced but well concealed life-form was discovered on our red planet. It was not hostile though it seemed that way to begin with and many people died before we properly understood what we were dealing with. But these matters I've covered elsewhere and because of what happened, Mars, by then a going concern for its human population, gained her independence, no longer to be ruled as a collection of colonies by diverse commercial interests on Earth but as an integrated trading partner. And we had as president, elected overwhelmingly, a man who had dedicated much of his working life to the colonies and oversaw the expansion of our own base, Novamerica Five, where he still resides. I could understand if Joe van Allen, a grey-haired, tall and slightly stooping man decided to calculate his age in Martian years because some claim that back on Earth he'd be well over a hundred even though he looks no more than sixty something. You may have realised by the name that Novamerica Five was one of the bases established by the UAS, the United American States, but no one after independence got around to renaming most of them, regardless of who they once belonged to. I use the term, bases, to describe our communities but that is out of habit: some of those so-called bases have grown to resemble small towns, including that from which Joe holds office.

I was piloting wingships much of the time, carrying cargo and personnel, this before the new propulsion system developed on Earth put turbine powered wingships, as well as interplanetary rockets, out of business. Flying long distances about our planet suited me then because on many occasions I would be alone with my thoughts. I'd become absorbed with the scenery by day, which I populated with my own fantasies, and the stars at night that had me dreaming of what might lie out there. Pilots were of course unnecessary but personnel travelling from place to place preferred to see someone who appeared to be in charge; someone who would listen to their complaints. Like a good many others, I chose to remain on Mars for the kind of freedom and opportunities not so readily available on bustling, overcrowded and overregulated Earth.

Joe, our president, has long been a close friend and proved a father figure to me. He pulled a fast one over me a few short years back, not long before we faced the near disaster to which I just referred. Figuring I'd been unattached for too long, Joe matched my time schedules at base with visits by a young Swedish woman with long, corn-blond hair and an appealing, blue-eyed smile. She was a planetary scientist then working on Mars for the Europeans, her name, Karin Blomdahl. She often would show up when I was with Joe in one of the biodome cafés then Joe would find some reason to leave us alone together. By the time I'd realised what he was about it was too late, I was hooked. As things turned out I didn't blame him, no; at least she was genuinely as young and attractive as she looked and very soon other people around the base were commenting upon what they saw as my good fortune. I'll admit now, she's the best thing that ever happened to me and we've been through more dangers together than we could ever have anticipated. And that was not to end. Karin had been away from base for much of the time undertaking research for a project in which we and others were soon to become deeply involved.

Until recent events took over, Joe had wanted to press forward his plans for the first Mars museum, a pet project of his ever since our independence and one he'd asked me to help organise. The surface of Mars was littered with landers and rovers sent out from Earth, some dating way back to the nineteen seventies and I had already undertaken survey work. His idea was to have collected the most important of these by suitable means then place them on display under a biodome in one of our equatorial regions, or perhaps in an extension of some kind at our own base. Okay, there would never be hoards of visitors as would be the case on Earth, but the museum would reinforce our identity and represent human preoccupation with, and eventually the colonisation, of Mars. Joe was convinced Earth would demand some of these relics back but I couldn't see him allowing that. True that when on Titan we had recovered the Huygens lander by request of the Europeans but no one was going to try and live on Titan; at least no one in their right mind. There might, though, be temporary visits from anyone involved in the otherwise automated recovery of hydrocarbons from its frigid methane seas.

With time to spare, Karin and I were taking lunch in one of the smaller biodome cafes beneath a cluster of trees and away from the busy central pathway and fountain area. Close by fluttered colourful birds which, like the less obvious insect community, were all programmed to interact with, pollinate and help maintain our plant life but in most cases never to leave the biodome through any of its airlocks. The spiderbots, bots, spiders or whatever people wanted to call them, were allocated to keeping things tidy at ground level and were occasionally seen to scurry by with antennae waving. Playing their role, too, were the more obvious and openly friendly rodent-like creatures with soft fur and big brown eyes. Karin joked about my treating one as a pet since it would occasionally come running over and play at being affectionate when we entered the biodome.

After a stroll that day, arm in arm around the biodome perimeter path, we stopped for a time to gaze out across the sunlit Martian desert. We decided to take our minds off forthcoming events with the use of virtual reality and wander around the Uffizi gallery in Florence. Yes, you could find yourself back almost anywhere on Earth if the mood took you, without the crowds, unless you wanted to call them in as well. These facilities, available to all at every base, made living on Mars a lot easier for some. We were making our way through the biodome main airlock into the administration area when my left earlobe pinged. I reached to touch it and Joe's voice came through. 'Hi Brett, sorry to cut in when you're both down there relaxing but maybe you could get around to my office some time soon.'

'Sure,' I replied, 'We were off to Italy for one of our art trips but we can do that another time. Be with you in a couple of minutes.'

'That'll be great. I knew you'd be with Karin and seeing you together will be of prime importance - and the coffee will be on.'

'I take it that was Joe,' Karin smiled, 'and he wishes to see us both – yes?'

'He sure does and he'll want to swap updates on what we've learned and from you in particular. We can satisfy our artistic urges later.'

Yes, there were matters afoot that would sideline Joe's plans for the museum. We headed up to the next floor and along the passage to Joe's office, now his centre of planet-wide communications. There the door stood ajar. The first president of a united Mars he might be but Joe, unassuming as always, was not one to keep his friends and co-workers at bay. We entered to find him gazing through the Armaplast screen, this another material developed for use on Mars as well as elsewhere, and out across the runway where the wingships, including my own, used to arrive and depart. With the new propulsion systems, those days were largely gone so a good part of our runway, as with most of those on Mars, no longer needed to be cleared of wind-blown sand.

Joe turned and smiled, 'Hi, you two,' and gestured for us to sit. 'Coffee right now?' he asked, easing down to face us. He needn't have asked because we never turned down the offer. The machine close by was already bubbling and ready to dispense what we asked for. Also close by was that ornate nineteenth century mechanical clock of Joe's that kept time, so he claimed, with his home town back on Earth. He boasted that it was the only one of its kind on Mars and no one doubted that. It might have been useless here anyway as the Martian day is twenty four hours and thirty-seven minutes long. As the coffees slid over to us the clock pinged five times and that had me wondering if any other old clocks like it, in the appropriate time zone all those millions of kilometres away on Earth, were right then doing the same thing. Joe appeared relaxed but Karin and I knew this was to be no easygoing chat about his museum project.

'Let's go over once more what we know about this mysterious world,' he began. 'We'd all heard about a large object people for some time thought was hanging about way beyond our outer planets. Astronomers back on Earth had for long speculated about a ninth body, a so-called Planet X, that some claimed was responsible for minor disturbances in the orbits of Neptune and Pluto. They spent a great deal of time searching but as no one ever found anything like that, interest on Earth waned.' Turning his attention fully to Karin he added, 'but due mainly to your efforts we here on Mars *did* find something, didn't we.'

'We or our system certainly did,' she agreed, 'and it turned out Planet X really does exist. Ever since you assigned me to it my small team and I have continued to gather as much information as possible. Poor Brett here must have been wondering for a time why I'd been up at the space station observatory for days on end.'

'That's right,' I said, 'but I appreciate you had your duties and on such occasions I had to play the innocent bystander.'

'Well not for much longer,' said Joe. 'Karin, bring us both up to date; there will be a few things I'm still in the dark about though I'm sure by now you'll have passed the latest details to Brett.'

Karin finished her coffee, glanced at me then began, 'Okay, earlier this year, after our observatory received its final upgrades, we learned quite a bit more about this so-called Planet X.'

'And that's why I've had a few lonely nights,' I muttered.

'Sorry, Brett,' she smiled, but -.'

'No it's entirely my fault for pushing you on,' cut in Joe.

'Oh, he'll get over it won't you, dear,' she smiled, reaching to pat my arm.

Sure I'd get over it but for now, this Planet X, as I'd already learned from Karin, had never been a true part of our Solar System. In other words it's what we'd call a rogue planet, one torn from orbit around its parent sun, maybe by another passing star, then left to drift alone through the frigid void of empty space.

'For a long time' resumed Karin, 'well before anyone came to Mars, attention had been focussed more upon the furthest reaches of the universe as well as the moons of our outer planets where primitive life forms were eventually discovered. But here on Mars, because our orbit takes us somewhat closer to the outer limits of our system, we were able to look deeper into the Kuiper Belt, that hoard of icy rocks and asteroids beyond Neptune that sweep around our sun between thirty and over sixty times further out than Earth. What we found close to the edge of this was our mystery planet. It's obscured part of the time so we had to look long and hard but now we have the basic statistics. Our Planet X is at present well over sixty times further out from the sun than is Earth – that's around ten thousand million kilometres, which means light from the sun takes around nine hours to reach it as against only eight minutes for Earth and an average of thirteen for Mars. I say at present because although it has an orbit which, if stable, would give it a year of around five-five-eight Earth years, that orbit is far from stable. Planet X is brushing the very edge of our solar system and ready to begin its outward journey.'

'But for how long,' Joe asked, 'd'you think this rogue planet has been hanging around our back yard? I understand it's a fairly recent arrival.'

'We can't be precise right now,' she replied, 'but only years and probably not many. What surprises me is that its approach was never detected; perhaps because it was in the same plane as the Kuiper Belt. It looks to be a little greater than Earth-size at just over thirteen thousand kilometres diameter but with a slightly shorter rotation period of just over twenty-one and a half hours. It's of slightly lower mass but anyone standing there would feel little difference in the gravity because that's only some ten percent less than on Earth. Average surface temperature hovers a little above minus two hundred Celsius so whatever seas it once had will lie frozen, with water ice set strong as steel.'

'Has Mars sounding like the Mediterranean,' I remarked.

'Doesn't it so,' she continued, 'The feedback we're getting would suggest as well that Planet X is still tectonically active with at least the volcanic activity of Earth and it has a stronger magnetic field. The mainly nitrogen atmosphere is only a little thinner than Earth's but the fact that conditions there are not cold enough for this to freeze tells us Planet X is giving out sufficient heat of its own. We detected also traces of oxygen, methane and most importantly dimethyl sulphide.'

'Dimethyl sulphide?' I muttered.

'Yes, dear, dimethyl sulphide in case you've forgotten. This is strongly associated with living organisms which makes it quite possible higher life forms once *did* exist there.'

'Are you saying there could have been *intelligent* life,' Joe asked.

'Maybe things that found clever ways of killing each other like they did on Earth?' I added.

'Yes, Brett,' she responded with mock disapproval, 'so I hope you're taking all of this in.'

'Of course,' I shrugged.

'So what kind of life might be or have been possible there?' asked Joe.

'Yes, what kind of life,' Karin replied. 'Right now we can only guess. There are, of course, no transmissions of any kind and perhaps never were. The planet is, or was Earth-like and many of the most hostile places on Earth and beyond do support life even if we regard much of it as pretty basic. What we've so far discovered about our Planet X is quite amazing but it throws up far more questions than answers. So think, if intelligent life *did* evolve there it's possible that when this planet was cast adrift from its parent star the inhabitants might have taken measures to preserve their kind – and if that was so, how and for how long did they succeed? That really *is* why we need to go there.'

'Very well' said Joe. 'But now I must make it clear to you both - if we're going to get to Xenonia, Earth is still to be involved. More coffee anyone?'

'Get to -!' I queried, as my cup refilled. 'Even with Orion, the ship that took us to Titan, this would involve one hell of a time. And what did you just call it – Xenonia? Who proposed *that* name?' Karin looked as puzzled as I must have; Xenon was - is after all an inert gas like neon or argon.

Joe, leaning back in his chair, smiled sheepishly and replied, 'Well, er, I did. Back on Earth as well as here some people might call this kind of thing Planet X but that is so clichéd I figured we ought to come up with something better. A name like Xenonia was long ago proposed for another Kuiper Belt object but they later ditched it. Xenon, being a non-reactive gas, was once regarded as strange. The name itself is derived from the ancient Greek word for a stranger and from that we derive the modern term, 'xenophobia,' a fear of strangers, and a stranger is what this intrusive world is – a stranger not all that far outside our Solar System in astronomical terms. But I'm open to ideas if either of you have any of your own.'

'I think it's a perfectly good name,' smiled Karin, 'and I see no reason to change it. What do you say, Brett?'

'Sure, I'll go along with that, Joe, but why is Earth to be involved and though I'm game for anything you want me to take on how d'you expect anyone or anything from Mars or Earth to get to that far out in realistic time? Even if it had the resources of Titan and wasn't about to drift off somewhere else the sheer distance would make exploitation impractical. Why don't we send a dozen or so bots out there to take a general survey from orbit then maybe drop down to the surface for a closer look?'

'You'll see,' replied Joe, 'when I bring you up to date with my side of things. Let's consider first what we already know: the discovery of how to harness and reverse the effect of that long time mystery force called Dark Matter gave us the ability, in effect, to concentrate, to reverse and employ gravity itself as a means of propelling vessels through space with the aid of modified hyperdrives. Capable as she was, Orion was going to be updated because technology is moving as quick as it ever did. The UAS was already planning an update of Orion when you and your team were heading out to Titan. But the UAS is in a political tangle after their elections with Brazil threatening to pull out of the Union because they don't see eye to eye with the new president in Washington. It was always a pretty shaky affair anyway but it won't deter their interest in Planet X. Meanwhile, and this is not public knowledge even on Earth, development of *their* new hyperdrive has stalled for a time and that's allowed the Europeans to come up with something even more advanced. Trouble is *they* don't yet have anything to match Orion. She was a UAS project they hoped to latch into but we kept hold of her when you returned from Titan. So *we* have the fully equipped and well tested deep space vehicle and the Europeans have their new hyperdrive intended for a home in the likes of Orion with at least two more hyperdrives nearing completion.'

'*Two* more?' I queried.

'Yes but I'll get around to that in a minute or so. A while back I, with the approval of the heads of all main communities on Mars, concluded our final agreement with the European Federation. I'd been in confidential, that is encrypted talks with them for some time. What we agreed is to be implemented with utmost haste since they believe the Russians and the Asians may soon be hot on our tail and in particular the UAS, though about them there's been nothing more said of late and that has me wondering. The Europeans are to ship the two additional hyperdrives out here by cargo vessel together with a crew of three nominated to join you. They agreed that we would install the first hyperdrive inside Orion in a power core designed by ourselves to accommodate it. This can be done right here wholly within our own facilities. The cargo ship has an older version so we'll then fit her out with the second drive.'

'Why don't they fit out the cargo ship back on Earth since it's theirs?' I asked.

'Because, so they tell me, we will have solved any problems when doing so with Orion. What they might have meant is, they think we ought to be doing more since we'll be getting the initial publicity through yourselves now they don't have access to Orion. The third completed hyperdrive is being installed inside what they refer to as their service vessel as this was designed from the very beginning to accept it and to accompany Orion if they'd had the opportunity. The service vessel contains a laboratory, a basic materials plant from which to manufacture additional food supplies should that prove necessary plus a general supplies and basic accommodation unit. This vessel does not, of course, have Orion's capabilities for exploration and overall control nor is it, unlike the cargo vessel, designed to carry a crew in long term comfort. Okay, we've gone this far except for one more thing we haven't touched upon yet.'

Joe looked at us both in anticipation of the inevitable and vital question I'd already touched upon so I asked, 'Yes, we were saying it takes light itself nine hours to reach Xenonia from the sun so how long is it going to take us even with updated hyperdrive technology? Still a *very* long time I imagine.'

'Not so, Brett,' declared Joe, raising a hand to emphasise the point. 'Performance with the new drives will be increased *dramatically*. With Mars in the right position, as we soon will be, and the fleet following an arced trajectory above the plane of our planetary system; a course plotted to avoid anything that might get in the way, you could make Xenonia's orbit from Mars in less than forty hours.'

'Less than forty hours!' I responded. 'Why, that must be getting on for – for -!'

I had really no idea right then what it might be getting on for but I noticed Karin thinking hard with eyes closed, one finger raised and lips moving slightly. She was pretty good at working this kind of thing out and moments later she announced, 'I make that not far off a hundredth the speed of light – yes?'

'Not far off a hundredth the speed of light,' I muttered, downing the last of my coffee. I recalled some of those old movies where people travelled at light speed and more. Perhaps we were heading that way.

'That's it,' grinned Joe, pulling open his drawer. 'Not far off a hundredth the speed of light so I say we drink to that with something stronger than coffee.'

Among the other necessities of life we manufactured on Mars was included a pretty good bourbon, with which Joe and I had some familiarity. Karin was not about to turn it down, either, as fresh glasses appeared, followed by the flask. Joe poured each of us a generous measure. I now had a more extensive picture of the command Joe had proposed to me a while back and I realised to pull it off we'd be making history in a big way.

'Stealing the show from the UAS,' added Joe, raising his glass, 'was to be the Europeans and therefore *our* main priority with joint kudos even if Europe might somehow end up claiming the lion's share. But like I implied a minute or so back, there may be more to what's going on Earthside than I know. With the planets being presently where they are, the cargo vessel and crew will be here in nine days with the service vessel sent ahead to arrive in under one day. She'll wait in Mars orbit close to the space station where she can hang about until the six of you show up there. I figured out that would be more convenient than having her get in the way of things around here. When the time comes all three units, Orion, the cargo ship and the service vessel will cluster together as one unit in Mars orbit. On departure they will be held in the combined fields of their drives but controlled as one unit from Orion. This will maintain the whole assembly through acceleration at this end and deceleration at the other until Xenonia orbit is established. There they will decouple after which each will take on its own role. Orion will be capable of deep level searches below the planet's surface so that keeps a crucial part of the operation under your control, Brett. Orion herself will be carrying all the life support basics plus, in her lower cargo bay, one of our smaller ground vehicles – still able to accommodate six people but without some of the luxuries enjoyed by those we use for long distances on Mars. The GV will be insulated to avoid melting or vaporising whatever she's travelling over and will have more than adequate room to carry a couple of the spiderbots answerable only to you and Karin unless you decide to nominate one of the others. Orion will retain two of the bots on board as back-ups. When required she will also deploy up to twenty so-called Apollo satellites, each able to generate a powerful light source from low orbit. They will be controlled in their entirety or in smaller numbers by yourselves from Orion or from the ground vehicle. They'll brighten up selected locations on Xenonia to help you admire the scenery, if there's any to admire, that is.'

'It sounds as though we'll need our very lives brightening up on a totally sunless world,' mused Karin.

'Orion,' Joe continued, 'will also be carrying two of the helicopter skimmers able to access the surface as they did on Titan if the GVs can't be used. With the hyperdrives unloaded from the cargo ship down here, the skimmers will be transferred from Orion to her before she heads for Mars orbit because being a cargo ship she is better suited for the kind of operation we have in mind. Either skimmer will be delivered and collected in the lower atmosphere by the cargo ship under Orion's control. Both of the skimmers can be flown by either of you with one being a back-up and they will as you know be able to land on most level areas.' Joe downed the remains of his bourbon then as his old clock chimed again he said, 'Okay, d'you both have more questions while I pour us another drink?'

'How's the ground vehicle getting to the surface?' Karin asked.

'Ah, yes, Orion will deliver and collect the GV and crew via her own grappling system,' Joe replied. 'She's well equipped to do that.'

'How much a say in this operation will the team from Earth hope to have?' I asked, pushing my glass forward. 'After all, without their hyperdrives we wouldn't be going anywhere so distant.'

'Nor would they without our research work and advanced planning,' Joe responded. 'They'll have their own programme to follow but you, Brett, will remain in overall charge as before with Karin as second in command. I agreed they'd have control over use of the service vessel since it is wholly theirs but you can override that should you consider it necessary.'

'Some back on Earth must be resentful about Mars leading the way,' said Karin. 'D'you anticipate any problems with the people coming over to join us?'

'I can only hope not,' he answered, tilting the flask, 'but now's a good time for me to tell you both who they are and what I know of them before you meet face to face. Franz Bergmann appears to be the big man with the right connections. He looks around forty-five and that's his true age. He's worked for the European Federation as well as for the UAS of late and has been shuttling back and forth between the two so it's not entirely clear to me where his affiliations lie. It looks like Bergmann muscled in at the last minute to take the place of someone else in their crew but I've heard no explanation as to why. He was, however, in charge of the team responsible for the hyperdrive and its subsequent development so maybe that's the reason he's so keen to get in on the act. Bernard Campbell is a long established geophysicist and climate expert. He's seen forty five Earth years but has himself looking thirty-something. The third member of their team is Melina Montaigne and she *is* interesting. Forty-two Earth years according to her profile but in the images they beamed over she looks around twenty years younger. I traced her back to one of the universities in Europe as it was they who nominated her but then it all went blank. She specialises in life science and it's claimed by some sources she's able to sense the feelings and emotions of others to an unprecedented degree. The original reason given being that she's on hand to monitor team compatibility during long journeys and foresee any problems before they arise. Could be there's more to it than that because looking after the wellbeing of the crew is Orion's job as we know.'

'You're not saying she could be some sort of telepath, are you, Joe?' queried Karin. 'That kind of thing's been checked out often enough in the past but never gained much publicity.'

'Er, well I'm not sure what I'm saying because in her case I'm relying in part upon hearsay. A great deal of her working past seems to be a closely guarded secret so who knows. Like the others she'll be screened when she arrives on Mars and hopefully we'll know if she isn't fully human or even if she's legal. But then most of us can have our external senses enhanced, can't we – that's why spectacles and hearing aids are ancient history.'

'Well I don't want her staring into my head,' I responded, 'any more than I had Orion monitoring my heartbeat and other bodily functions on the Titan trip.'

'That I understand, Brett, but there isn't much more I can say about Melina or the others until they're actually with us. We have our agreement with the Europeans and that being so we have to accept the three as they are unless they pose some kind of threat to ourselves or the project. You'll get to know them soon enough; well before we have our show on the move.'

We chatted further, finished our drinks and agreed we would get together again the following day. After the meeting Karin and I planned to discuss all necessary procedures we'd have to deal with in Mars orbit when the time arrived. Later that afternoon we found ourselves once more in the biodome and heading along the perimeter path toward the west side. We'd abandoned all thoughts of our art excursion but as we stood to watch sunset over the desert, chimes sounded to warn of a scheduled rainfall. Yes, we had real rain - rain that fell from above, that is, whereas some smaller bases still relied upon hydroponics to keep their plant life healthy. Most people, those who wanted to avoid getting wet, would head for shelter at a café or to the main biodome airlock but we decided to remain where we were; hand in hand beneath a tree where we hoped to stay reasonably dry. Our rain, a heavy shower, didn't last long but it left a wonderful fresh tang in the air. By then the sun had set behind a range of hills to leave an ethereal violet glow above the horizon. Still illuminated in the upper atmosphere there hung a linear sweep of thin white frozen carbon dioxide clouds that glowed bright against a deepening saffron sky.

'So beautiful out there in its way, don't you think?' Karin whispered, squeezing my hand.

Beautiful yes, I wouldn't disagree with that, but now my thoughts turned to that sunless world to which we would soon enough be headed. A world of never ending night.

Chapter 2 - Those from Earth

The newly commissioned service vessel was well on its way from Earth and soon to reach Mars orbit. Meanwhile Karin and I would have time to relax as well as attend further talks with Joe. Much welcomed at those follow-up meetings was a person we knew well, her name Sunita Chandra, a slim and attractive woman with long, raven-black hair. She'd originally been checked out by Joe as being in her late-thirties but has herself looking ten or so Earth years younger.

Sunita, a biochemist, had been with us on our visit to Titan where she'd been responsible for essential, and as it turned out, potentially lifesaving research. On returning to Earth she had opted to abandon her employment there and take up her work on Mars. This was especially welcomed by Joe who saw her as another addition to our ever expanding pool of skilled and enthusiastic people eager to explore more open-ended opportunities and challenges on the red planet, still regarded by some back on Earth as a kind of frontier land. Flown over by sub-orbital shuttle from duties on the other side of Mars, Sunita would be in on further discussions with Joe and ourselves, sometimes in his office but more often in one of our biodome cafes.

***

The four of us were up in Joe's office that morning, gazing out to the landing area when the cargo vessel, at that distance a featureless metal sliver, appeared as expected in the sky above nearby hills. The landing area, part cleared earlier from the ever present wind-blown sand, looked busier than it had for some time with a trio of rocket shuttles from other Mars bases and a pair of tracked ground vehicles of our own standing close by. All of these had brought in engineers to help us in getting our act together. In case you were wondering, the Mars based shuttles were and would remain rocket powered for the foreseeable future since they were too small by far to accommodate a hyperdrive.

The cargo ship carrying those people who were to join us was drifting closer to the service vessel from Earth already in orbit close by our space station. Our engineers had worked out well in advance a way of adapting the cargo vessel to take her replacement hyperdrive. While down here she would, as Joe earlier explained, take on board our two skimmers as well as other equipment.

'You any idea at present, Joe,' I asked, 'how likely are we to stay ahead of any opposition?'

'The Europeans assure me they're still confident in that respect,' he replied, 'but I'm sure the UAS has a finger in the pie. As for how long we stay ahead, they're not as optimistic as they originally were. A month in Earth time, maybe, was suggested and that being so we figured it would give us ample opportunity, even taking into account that needed to integrate the new drives into Orion's power core and that of the cargo ship. But as we know, Xenonia isn't going to hang around.'

We stood in silence to watch the incoming ship drift slowly down. In spite of my own experiences I, like most people here, still found this an odd sight because rocket power had, until recently been the only way to deliver and collect people travelling between Mars and Earth.

The vessel steadied a couple of meters above the ground and as the boarding ramp descended three of our own personnel in white pressure suits were stepping across to meet our visitors. Three likewise attired figures appeared at the top of the ramp, each holding a small case, and Joe said, 'Okay, let's head off down there and show those Earthlings how much we appreciate their arrival.'

'Are you still to have them security scanned as they come through?' asked Karin as we left the office.

'Damned right I am,' muttered Joe.

It only occurred to me then, as we were about to meet the three, that Sunita had appeared somewhat reserved when the subject of Franz Bergmann entered our conversation. She'd expressed interest in Bernard Campbell and in Melina Montaigne but not the other man although it seemed of little importance at the time. On entering the well-lit reception area we could see straight into the main airlock as the metal inner doors had of late been replaced by transparent Armaplast. Sunlight flooded through as the outer doors slid open to reveal six waiting figures silhouetted against the pale saffron sky. They stepped inside, stamping powder-fine red sand from their boots then stood to peer through at us whilst a muffled roar told them the dust extractors were doing their job. As pressure within the airlock reached optimal level those inside were loosening their helmets and the inner doors were opening. Two of the crewmen left them and hurried by while the third ushered the new arrivals in our direction, helmets and cases clasped in their hands. Joe moved forward and introduced himself with a genial 'Welcome to Mars!' before adding to the crewman, 'Take these folks across to stow their pressure suits then we can have ourselves a proper introduction.'

Ten minutes later the three, clad in their crew suits, returned to join us. We knew, of course, who was who regardless of their suit tags but as Joe had kept to a personal minimum his earlier, covert conversations with Earth, the rest of us were to speak with them for the first time. The customary verbal greetings with handshaking began as Joe slapped my shoulder and announced, 'This is Commander Anderson, Brett to most people - you'll know him I'm sure from past news on Earth. He's all set to head our expedition out to Xenonia.' Bergmann managed for me an off-the-shelf smile. 'Karin Blomdahl,' Joe continued, 'you may also recognise. She is our top planetary scientist and Brett's second in command. Sunita Chandra was, back on Earth, a renowned bio and organic chemistry specialist and we're extremely fortunate to have her working with us here on Mars.'

All of us affected a smile, including Sunita, but when Bergmann took her hand with what I noted as lingering grasp and intent stare, her smile faded.

'We're most pleased to be here,' announced Bernard Campbell. 'I visited Mars before the troubles you had and I looked forward to this time around, especially as the journey time on this occasion was very much reduced and we had gravity.'

'And I so looked forward to it as my first visit,' said Melina Montaigne. 'I know you have wonderful gardens within your biodomes but I did not expect the smell of flowers to reach me so soon.'

'My first visit also,' added Franz Bergmann. 'I must take care not to hurry too quickly in your lower gravity.'

'Don't want to bang our head on anything, do we,' grinned Joe.

I wondered at the time why Bergmann would want to hurry anywhere. With the greetings ritual finished, Joe said, 'Okay let's make our way up to my office where we can relax and check out the best coffee on the planet.'

As we turned to leave the reception area with me following Joe and Karin, I had more time to weigh up our new company. Bernard Campbell was of average build, round faced, brown-eyed and dark haired. Following him closely, fairer haired Franz Bergmann was of slimmer build, but sterner, more angular features and sharp, pale blue eyes. Though given opportunity on the journey over, he was still not adjusted to Mars gravity and needed to take more than a little care with his footsteps. With Joe's earlier words in mind I wondered also about his association with the UAS who he knew in their extra-planetary dealings and why he'd been allowed to jump the queue before leaving Earth. Sunita chatted to the slim and coolly attractive Melina Montaigne whose long dark hair was clipped back to expose gold earrings set with red gemstones. Such adornments were less common here on Mars where practicality reigned and concern for fashion was yet to become the high priority it had always been on Earth. I noted also her dark-eyed expression; one of calm concentration.

'Your biodome,' said Bernard, glancing back at me as we ascended the steps to the floor above, 'we were looking down on it as we came in. What an amazing sight it is – yes, *what* a sight! You must be concerned at times over meteorites - or are you?'

'Yes,' put in Franz,' what if one of these punches a hole through while there are many people inside? I was thinking as we came down; your atmosphere is too insubstantial to stop most of what would burn up in the air above Earth.'

'Well if it's a smallish hole,' answered Joe, turning to him and gesturing upwards as we stepped along the corridor to his office, 'the Bioplast would grow in soon enough to fill it. A bit larger and our bots would activate standby material to take up and seal the damage before too much air escaped. Since independence we've installed emergency oxygen masks at designated points around nearly all of our biodomes so I guess most people would make it to safety unless the situation proved catastrophic. Other than that, we have the necessary systems to warn of incoming objects likely to endanger life but so far none of these has been activated.'

'It is not a risk I would be happy to take,' Bergmann responded, peering momentarily upwards.

That had me thinking afresh about our biodomes. Used to these as I am, I still regard as a tremendous achievement what some out here take for granted.

'Are you trying to cheer us up, Franz,' Karin asked. 'If you are then think about the millions on Earth who live close to some pretty dangerous volcanoes and earthquake zones. At least we don't have any of those to worry about.'

'I am sorry,' he replied, tugging to straighten the slightest of creases in his crew suit, 'but a meteor strike is possible, I think.'

'It's not a good idea to be pessimistic living on Mars,' I said as we entered Joe's office. 'Better to look on the bright side or sideline yourself into a favourite dream fantasy like people do on Earth as well as out here.'

'Sit down,' invited Joe, 'and just tell that machine by my desk what kind of coffee you hope she'll give you before the next meteorite wipes us all out.'

Only Melina declined the offer and as I reached for my coffee I glanced out to see our low-loader, equipped with lifting gear, angling around below the cargo ship with a pressure-suited crew assembled to assist in the unshipping of our precious new hyperdrives. It caught Franz Bergmann's attention, too. He stared a while longer but made no comment. One of he hyperdrives would be taken through our service building to where, on the other side, DSV Orion waited. Bernard and Melina were both surprised and amused by Joe's ancient clock and commented on it accordingly though Franz offered the treasured timepiece no more than a puzzled glance.

Our meeting in Joe's office, intended only to allow each party to gain further familiarity with the other, was eventually curtailed when two orderlies showed up to conduct our new arrivals to their allocated quarters.

'You'll all have local time,' said Joe as they turned to leave, 'so come down to the biodome main airlock for seven-thirty and we'll have a bite to eat at one of our cafes.'

Now free to talk Karin asked the inevitable question: 'The security scans, Joe, can we see if they revealed anything of interest?'

'We sure can,' he responded, ordering the Armaplast window to dim and calling up the information we wanted on the wall close by his desk. I'm not sure what we expected, or at least what *I* expected, but we all were eager to see the results. Bernard Campbell we checked out first: He has some bone modifications and improved hearing ability but nothing out of the ordinary. Franz Bergmann has little to show other than those standard health enhancements common on Earth or on Mars. Melina Montaigne was not so easy to figure out.

'She has a built-in resistance to scanning,' said Joe, 'and from the feedback it looks like somehow she'll know we tried. But as our system here at number five is pretty good there's still a certain amount we can ascertain.'

'She appears remarkably healthy in body,' observed Sunita, peering at the results, 'though your system is telling us there are enhancements to the frontal lobe of her brain and elsewhere deeper within, particularly the amygdala.'

'The amygdala?' I queried.

'Yes,' replied Sunita, 'it is the main processing centre for emotions and connects to memories, learning and other senses. Then there are her eyes – they are not artificial but certainly modified and may possess greater resolving power even than our own.'

'But from what I see of it,' remarked Karin, 'the scan tells us little more.'

'All of this,' said Sunita, 'must, be linked with this supposed ability of hers you mentioned earlier; to sense the feelings and emotions of others and predict any difficulties. That might be to our advantage.'

'Ought we not be a little suspicious, Joe?' I asked.

'Difficult to say, Brett. You don't want any problems but for most of the journey she'll be out of touch with Earth like the rest of you. If I had to keep an eye on anyone at all it might be that guy Bergmann. No more than a gut feeling, I guess. Maybe I ought to have scanned the few things they were carrying with them but I didn't at the time imagine there would be anything to worry about.'

I felt inclined to agree with Joe's remark about Bergmann but it was this that triggered the following comment from Sunita. 'Perhaps I should have mentioned this sooner although it seemed of no importance until now. I worked with Franz Bergmann for a short time at a research unit in Europe. That was two years ago and well before he began his trips to America. He paid more attention to me than I wished; far more in fact, but that ceased for a time when I moved to a different unit.'

Well I couldn't blame the guy for paying attention to her but his presence *was* something of a coincidence.

'He tried to contact me later,' she continued. 'On several occasions he persisted; he even had other people contact me on his behalf but I did not respond. Having dedicated himself to hyperdrive development I think he originally wanted me as a kind of appendage but I saw it later as becoming an obsession.'

'Okay,' said Joe, 'that's unfortunate considering how much time you'll be spending together but there's nothing – no, nothing at all we can do about it now. Sit close to me in the café and I'll keep my eye on him.'

'Orion will sense anything untoward will she not?' queried Karin. 'Or maybe Melina will.'

'If Orion does,' I said, 'it'll be reported directly to me. I'll have no one causing problems under my command.'

***

The next few days offered an opportunity for relaxation with all six of us free to enjoy the pleasures of our biodome, from time to time accompanied by Joe. Sunita avoided eye contact with Franz Bergmann except when they managed an occasional though brief exchange of words. I'd already noted by then how fussy the man seemed to be; the way he frequently adjusted the sleeves and collar of his crew suit and in particular the care with which he handled his food; as if a mistaken slip of the knife or fork might cause it to vanish. I told myself it shouldn't matter under the present or any other circumstances, particularly as the time for us to leave Mars was growing closer.

You may recall my mentioning Amalia Barbosa, our ambassador to the home planet and based most of the time at our primary space station. Amalia had her own discreet contacts in various locations on Earth. She and I had spoken recently of the forthcoming expedition and I looked forward to our meeting.

Orion had departed under her own control with the ground vehicle and was waiting now in orbit. Because her size prevented her docking directly with the space station, as had been the case with those earlier big rockets, we would go up there in one of our smaller rocket shuttles to save a time-consuming transfer in pressure suits, though until recently they had been required as a precaution. Sunita, Bernard, Melina and of course Karin and I were used to shuttle trips but Franz was not because the cargo ship had picked him up directly from Earth and he'd had an easy time of it in getting to Mars. We enjoyed an amiable enough breakfast beneath the biodome with Franz saying, 'Your shuttles must be very reliable and in use much of the time I take it.' His voice carried a hint of concern.

'We've not had too many deaths of late,' I muttered.

'Oh, Brett!' Karin exclaimed, turning from me to Franz. 'Take no notice of him; I assure you our shuttles are perfectly safe; I use them often as a part of my work to access our observatory and they're essential for base to base travel.'

Franz looked from me to Karin and forced a smile. It seemed increasingly odd to me that his placement with us had given him too little time to familiarise himself fully on Earth about our journey. Having done so would have made a lot of sense. Soon he must experience the thunder, vibration and g-force of rocket power though it would not last for long.

We separated to collect a few personal belongings then met up in one of our service areas wearing our white crew suits. From there we boarded a ground vehicle and crossed the runway in bright sunlight to where the shuttle waited like some great metallic insect ready to leap high. We entered the shuttle one at a time via the somewhat awkward flexible airlock extended from her to the GV. Once on board we were seated in a small crescent with safety belts secured and large, curved virtual window to give everyone a good view of what lay outside. 'Okay shuttle,' I announced, 'rendezvous with the space station as standard procedure.'

The rockets roared into life, the shuttle trembled and we watched red sand blasted away from beneath as she lifted off. I switched my attention to the others. Karin and Sunita were smiling at one another, Bernard peered down at our base as the buildings and biodome fell away. Melina appeared relaxed but this new experience for Franz had him gripping the arms of his seat with his eyes fixed hard upon the scene beyond. Right then I felt sorry for the guy. Well almost.

The rockets had become a steady, subdued rumble as we continued to climb. Visible like a ruptured abscess on the horizon was soon revealed the sprawling bulk of Mount Olympus, or at least one side of it, largest volcano in our solar system. Drifting into view also was more of the Tharsis Rise upon which stood another three giant volcanoes, Ascraeus, Pavonis and Arsia, with Pavonis straddling the red planet's equator. As we crossed the evening terminator to see a Mars bathed in darkness I looked directly at Franz and, hoping to quell his anxiety as we were by then in zero gravity, I said, 'You must have seen these images before you came over to us. They can't look any different.'

'That is so,' he responded dryly, 'no different as you say, but then I was not heading into space as we are now.'

'We'll soon be at the station,' Karin assured him.

'On my previous visit,' informed Bernard, 'It was by rocket *all* the way; from Earth directly to the surface of Mars.'

'A pleasure denied to me,' smiled Sunita. She glanced briefly at Franz and I had the feeling she experienced a degree of pleasure at the thought of his discomfort. Melina sat looking from one to the other, a hint of amusement touching her face.

Still rising though now at a shallow angle and drifting above the equator, the shuttle would soon level off at under a thousand kilometres altitude in readiness for rendezvous with the space station. A chime sounded, abstract images pulsed for attention and a voice announced, 'We will commence docking at the Isaac Newton space station in eight minutes. Please ensure all personal belongings are removed from this vessel when you leave.'

The images dissolved then in front of us materialised the space station a few kilometres ahead and rotating majestically against the stars. Anyone seeing it for the first time would get the impression of a giant silver cylinder consisting of huge joined-up ring segments floating above the rusted, scarred and cratered face of Mars. The station spun about its long axis, except for the cluster of interlocked, modular hexagonal structures close by that contained the observatory and various laboratories as well as a docking facility used until recently by some of the big rockets from earth. Suspended within the cylinder at one end was the service hub containing the power core together with a number of other utilities.

'I thought this was very impressive when looked at on Earth in simulation,' said Bernard, 'but actually being here, well, it's quite magnificent. How did your space station end up in its present form – this I never fully learned?'

'The service hub,' I replied, 'and first ring segment were sent out from Earth for assembly here in orbit during the earlier part of the last century as an international effort. It would have looked like a great wheel, rotating to simulate near to Mars gravity with more ring sections containing laboratories and living accommodation added over the decades. People assigned to the station lived and worked then as they still do between the pressurised inner and outer walls of the cylinder so the inner wall is their ceiling and the outer wall their floor. Many of the operations once undertaken here were transferred to the surface as the colonists became self-sufficient so now we end up with a piece of orbiting real estate partly unoccupied for much of the time. There were plans to convert some of it into an orbital hotel for Earth tourists but nothing came of that idea. Anyway, you're about to see how we get inside.'

Docking at the space station could be a weird, disorientating experience. As we passed by the rim to enter the illuminated interior of the cylinder, the station's control systems meshed with that of our own. This caused the shuttle to match her speed and direction to that of the rotating body whilst turning her about until she was perpendicular to the cylinder's axis of rotation with her stern facing the inner wall. We drifted toward the wall, which had now become our downward direction with the station's centrifugal motion giving us a new source of gravity. After that fancy piece of co-ordination we were docked and things began to feel as normal as anything could be under the circumstances. Bernard was obviously most impressed. The girls exchanged comments whilst Franz, though attentive and glancing at each of us in turn, in particular at Sunita, continued to look anxious.

'Wonder how he'll be feeling when we reach Xenonia,' I muttered to myself.

The access elevator housing telescoped upward from the inner wall of the station then clamped onto the airlock of our shuttle. The elevator, being pressurised, allowed for convenient access though it was necessary for us to descend in two parties of three with our small cases. We gathered in the plain but well-lit reception area, there to be greeted by broadly smiling Amalia and two crewmen. After introductions the crewmen would conduct Sunita and those from Earth to temporary quarters. 'We will all get together for something to eat in half an hour,' informed Amalia. Karin and I, as previously arranged, would accompany Amalia to her office. Amalia turned to Franz, Bernard and Melina, saying, 'Now we're inside a rotating system you need to walk steadily and don't hurry.'

Very considerate, I thought, as we turned to follow her, likewise with due care. Unlike most people, including myself and Karin, Amalia seemed happier based in orbit rather than down on the surface, perhaps more of an avid star gazer even than I had been when flying wingships. Her office, disturbingly homely and comfortable considering the location, was where she spent most of her working day. We'd agreed to keep our presence as low key as possible – away from most other people on the station, even though everybody must have ogled the cluster of vessels hanging there in space close by. As soon as we sat down she had one entire wall resolve as a virtual window showing that part of Mars, once more in sunlight, and the vessels in orbit close by us, image stabilised as if the station no longer rotated. Out there drifted Orion, the cargo vessel and the service vessel. This last comprised of three interconnected, flattened cylinders of equal size with the centre one protruding ahead of the outer two, the space behind it being filled by their presently independent hyperdrive. The left hand unit, as if viewed from above, was the laboratory. That in the centre was the materials processing plant and on the right was the section which we'd possibly need to draw upon for food and other supplies should our stay at Xenonia be prolonged. This vessel and the others would soon be clustered together, locked within the combined fields of their hyperdrives and ready to depart.

'How very impressive,' Amalia said. 'I never thought I'd see anything like this. I'm not sure I envy you though, going out to such a strange and distant place.'

'Perhaps it won't be too strange once we get there,' suggested Bernard, 'but for now we can only guess.'

'But this is an almost unknown world,' said Karin. 'There have been no prior missions, no orbiters and no landers but at least the travelling time won't be a problem.'

'That's so' I added, 'less than it was to reach Titan.

'But Titan, with her methane oceans,' said Amalia, 'is already becoming a commercial asset to Earth and Mars. From what you and in particular Karin have told me it seems you'll find nothing like that on Xenonia. Would it not have been better in the end to send intelligent probes? They could stay there and keep on sending back information even as Xenonoa drifts away from the Kuiper Belt.'

'Maybe so,' I answered, 'but I still think there's good reason for real people to go, otherwise what use are we, and this is possibly the only chance anyone will have before the planet returns to deep space. And talking of intelligent probes, as now they have to be, remember the problems they had back on Earth in the twenty-first century when artificial intelligence took a hold?'

'Quite,' said Karin, 'it began to look as though people were no longer needed and many felt threatened by it all. Yes, towards the end they *were* threatened. AI became a master rather than a servant and that's why human beings had to reinstate themselves in so many areas – sometimes by force.'

'Orion is designed to look after us without making demands,' I said, 'and our spiderbots will always do as they're told unless they're faced with unforeseen problems.'

'Then how about coffee from a machine that does as it's told,' smiled Amalia. 'Our coffee is at least as good as Joe's.'

'Don't *ever* let him hear you say that,' Karin smiled as Amalia gave orders to the machine.

'Have you gleaned anything more of interest from Earth lately?' I asked Amalia as the coffees appeared.

'I picked up something that leaked out from Washington only hours ago,' she replied. 'The European Federation and the UAS now have some kind of deal going related to your Xenonia project.'

'Oh, really, have you any idea what they're about?' I asked although I was but mildly surprised.

'Unfortunately not,' she answered, 'but it seems to involve high-ups on both sides of the Atlantic and Bergmann is, or certainly was, involved. That's why he was opted into their team at the last minute.'

'Are you going to question him, Brett?' asked Karin. 'I wouldn't be surprised if this so-called deal of theirs has been going on for some time.'

'Question him? No, at least not yet. The last thing I want is a bad start to this journey and there's enough suspicion hanging over the show already. If

I believed in omens I'd say it wasn't a good one. I'll have those well-meaning senses of Orion keep closer tabs on Franz as well as doing so myself whenever circumstances allow.'

'Perhaps we could make use of Melina,' Karin suggested.

She had a point but there was little to be gained in our embarking on further speculation over other members of our crew so Amalia returned instead to the main issue - Xenonia.

'You must be asking yourselves constantly what you might find there,' she said. 'It would be giving me sleepless nights, I know that.'

'I can't say we've had sleepless nights,' responded Karin. 'It doesn't help to dwell on the possibilities so far in advance as I admit we have time and time again. In spite of the encouraging feedback we've so far gained, Xenonia still might end up being a dead rock where no life of any significance or any life at all ever existed in spite of contrary indications.'

'Maybe so,' I agreed, 'but if nothing else there's at least plate tectonics resulting in a good few volcanoes to cheer things up.' Karin and I were tying to wind down our expectations of Xenonia but fuelled by Amalia's questioning they refused to go away. We continued in conversation a while longer until the time arrived when we were to rejoin the other four. As arranged by Amalia we met up with them in the station dining area where, once seated together, the machine dutifully dispensed those dishes required from our verbal orders; a big plus for at least this example of artificial intelligence. We sat around a while after eating with a motion-stabilised view of the stars spread over the ceiling as if there was no ceiling there at all. I was pleased to find conversation relaxed and amiable There was but little hint of tension discernable between Franz and Sunita. Her conversation was taken up more frequently with Bernard, who returned this with an occasional and none too discreet smile. We finished by deciding upon our rest periods during the voyage ahead then agreed it ought now to be our bedtime. As I mentioned earlier, there were a number of unoccupied areas on the space station so Sunita, Bernard, Melina and Franz could each select the quarters they most fancied with Karin and I taking ours. You might have forgotten you were inside a rotating system unless you rolled out of bed at night and hurried across the room too quickly at the wrong angle.

The space station by now was, as you may have realised, on the way to becoming an anachronism. Someday a different station would be built with the seemingly real gravity we would enjoy once we were back on board Orion.

After a notional night's sleep with programmed dreams came the notional morning followed by real breakfast, with Amalia joining us. She accompanied us afterwards to the airlock where, with our modest personal possessions, we passed through to board the shuttle for our short journey across to Orion. During the attention absorbing time it took the shuttle to manoeuvre, twisting and turning out of the space station, no one spoke. Below was a morning view of Mars. Watching the scene all about us seemed to impose a silence that Karin and I had no inclination to break. Minutes later we were docked with Orion and I stepped through the airlock with Karin to see the others through. As we assembled Orion announced, 'Welcome onboard! Your comfort and your safety will be my priority during our journey.'

'That'll be fine,' I responded. 'Please confirm you are fully programmed for our journey.'

'Of course - fully programmed and as always ready to depart at your command.'

'This is truly fascinating,' remarked Bernard, peering about.

'I sense Orion is scanning us as we stand here,' said Melina, her eyes lightly closed.

'Scanning us,' muttered Franz, glancing down at his briefcase. 'Is she, now.' He passed a tidying hand over his hair as he gazed uncomfortably upwards. He didn't know, of course, that he'd already been scanned by Joe on reaching our base.

Sunita glanced from Franz to me with a hint of amusement touching her face. Karin noticed it also then said, 'Let's show everyone to their quarters first then afterwards we can assemble on the control deck.'

Some twenty minutes later we were seated facing Orion's bow on what most people still call the control deck for want of a more suitable name. I recall that once it was referred to as the bridge. The area directly ahead of us appeared as if there was nothing between ourselves and deep space. This could be disconcerting unless you were used to it though it was alleviated, perhaps, by the information panel glowing to one side that showed our present situation. It would update constantly with location and speed once we were on our way. Karin and Sunita continued in conversation with the others as, or so it seemed to me, a means of mutual reassurance.

'Orion, you may proceed as planned!' I announced, 'but show us Mars in natural perspective for a while.'

The chatter ceased. Mars and a part of the space station appeared before us although they actually lay to our rear. A harsh, three-stroke chime told us we were about to leave orbit. For some moments nothing happened then the space station began to fall away. Then Mars, at first receding almost imperceptibly. I for one couldn't help but brace myself for a second or so in expectation of a tremendous G-force even though I knew there would be none. Instead we would all experience that oddest of sensations when the force field seized every molecule in our bodies as it did the entire, consolidated fleet. The scene on display before us was diminishing a little quicker and the sun had come into view. Then quicker still. I had Orion revert our view to what lay directly ahead; once again blackness, strewn with a myriad stars. With space ready to draw us further than ever before into its fearful vastness, our journey had begun.

Chapter 3 - Beyond Neptune

We were not expecting to see much of interest during the forty hour journey. We'd arc above the Asteroid Belt then over the orbits of those swollen bags of gas, Jupiter and Saturn then the two so-called ice giants, Uranus and Neptune, but we'd glimpse nothing of them since their orbital situations had them all too far away. Pluto in its wayward wanderings from the inner Kuiper belt to within the orbit of Neptune would also elude us but then all these outer worlds had been visited so many times by robot vessels over this and the previous two centuries that their absence would not prove too great a disappointment. And there was Saturn's moon, Titan, target for automated commercial vessels but one place Karin and I had no desire to encounter a second time. Space itself, as we observed, didn't offer a great deal in the way of novelty. The stars and constellations appeared little different than they did from Mars or Earth so under the benevolent gaze of Orion we could maybe take things easy with conversation and a little entertainment. Or so I thought at the time.

Our first meal onboard Orion, in the small dining area designed for six people, was a pleasant enough affair with relaxing music and gently flowing, restful forms that drifted, coiled and uncoiled slowly about the walls. The fact that Orion generated her own gravity was an asset beyond praise. The food and drinks dispenser I considered a triumph of modern technology. Improved somewhat since the Titan days to account for longer journeys, it seemed to satisfy us all with its varied offerings and verbal suggestions in a reassuring feminine voice. Maybe that was what had Karin ask Franz Bergmann, 'Are you finding this journey easier, now? You were not used to space travel at all, were you?'

Franz hesitated. Bernard and I looked on casually. Sunita peered down at her empty plate then glanced at Bernard while Karin and Melina stared at Franz in anticipation of his answer.

'That is so,' he answered at last, 'I am quite unused to true spaceflight although I have made a number of sub-orbital journeys on Earth. But as one responsible for our propulsion system and the main accompanying facilities I felt it necessary to see things all the way through.'

I thought it had to be more than that since there must have been many others involved including whoever it was stepped, or was pushed aside, to let him muscle in. I regretted even more not having questioned Franz Bergmann fully on his last minute appointment but now was not the time.

'You were busy enough when - after I knew you, were you not, Franz,' said Sunita with a hint of sarcasm, 'off from one side of the Atlantic to the other almost every week.'

'Pressure of work,' he responded, 'but you could have come with me; I did ask you did I not.'

'My work was important, too,' she responded, 'and it has been all the more satisfying since I moved to Mars.'

'I can see the appeal of Mars,' said Bernard, 'though I'm not sure there'd be much for me to get involved with there. At least not yet.'

'You have to turn your hand to other things apart from your main work,' I pointed out. 'Joe van Allen had me looking at ways to help create his pet project, the first space museum on Mars. I have to say I was rather looking forward to collecting and organising the exhibits; there are more than enough landers and ground vehicles lying around the place; far more than enough in fact.'

'The landers should all be returned to Earth,' declared Franz, 'because that is where they belong. There was talk of such a museum there well before Mars became independent.'

'Most of those intended to return to Earth by themselves did just that,' I responded, 'so the rest we keep.'

'We recovered the Huygens lander from Titan for the Europeans,' added Karin,' and that at some risk to ourselves.'

'So your people ought to be grateful we didn't hang onto that as well,' I informed him though I was no longer quite sure who his people were. Bergmann gazed coldly at me for a while but said nothing more on the subject.

'I followed all that you did on Titan,' said Melina. 'I feel it was very, how shall I say, eventful. Exciting perhaps?' Throughout this spell of chatter

Melina had until then said little although she had looked at everyone in turn and appeared to listen with keen interest.

'Oh, very exiting,' Karin smiled while pushing back her hair, 'if you like that kind of thing.'

'Yes, great fun,' I added, gazing at Franz. 'Pity it is we aren't passing close to Saturn otherwise we could drop you down there to take a close look.'

'Drop down to Titan,' reflected Bernard. 'From what I recall Orion made your journey there – even as this one, seem almost routine, yet we're hurtling through space at unprecedented speed and will be many times more distant from our home planets than anyone has ever been or ever could be until now.'

'I hope we will find enough of interest to make it all worthwhile,' remarked Sunita.'

'We've almost a couple of hours until our next rest period,' said Karin. 'Do we want to entertain ourselves on the control deck for a while?'

'Fine by me,' said Bernard.

Sunita and Melina were in agreement with Bernard but Franz said, 'Perhaps I will join you later but for now I will return to my quarters and listen to a little music – Bach perhaps.'

'Guess I'll spend a while in the gym,' I shrugged as we arose from the table.

'Now that sounds a good idea,' said Karin. 'I'll be along to join you later.'

We left the dining area and not wishing to appear neglectful I saw Bernard and the others to the control deck where we arranged to call up one of those ancient twentieth century movies that I'd heard were in vogue back on Earth. I made my exit and was passing our vessel's power core on my way to the gym when my left earlobe pinged. I reached to touch it and Orion's voice came, 'Brett, I have decrypted a message specifically for you from the Isaac Newton space station.'

That surprised me as we were by then much too far from Mars to hold meaningful dialogue, though Orion would frequently beam back our status to Joe van Allen. I reckoned the time delay by then must have been somewhere around three hours. 'Okay,' I responded, 'I'll listen to it now.'

Moments later I was hearing Amalia's voice. 'Brett, we detected an unidentified space vehicle crossing Mars orbit. It obviously originated from Earth but appears not large enough to be supporting any crew. We locked onto and tracked it via the station observatory and find its velocity matches your own so it must possess the latest hyperdrive. There is no doubt about it - you are being followed. Its trajectory, however, is lower than your own so that it will gradually catch up with you. That is as much as I can say for mow but Orion should be able to locate it also and relay information to me. Whatever happens I will be keeping Joe informed.'

That was quite a turn-up, especially since there were supposed to be only three of those newly developed drives in existence at the time – the ones we had powering our fleet. The gym could wait; I needed to think more about what was going on and have Orion check things out also. I was heading back to the control deck when Karin and Melina appeared before me in the corridor. 'Brett,' said wide-eyed Melina, 'you are in charge of this expedition and so it is with you and with Karin I must speak in private.'

'Sure, then I'll tell you what *I* just found out. Let's head to our quarters first, though.'

Once there in complete privacy Melina stood before us looking decidedly anxious. 'I believe,' she began, 'no, I am certain that Franz Bergmann is keeping important information about our project from myself and from Bernard. This I find of some concern because it may involve us all.'

'Just how far do your abilities go?' Karin asked her. 'They seem pretty keen to me.'

Melina hesitated then replied, 'That depends upon – I am not entirely sure; I find this difficult to explain.'

I put it to her, 'There has to be more to you being here than we've been led to believe, so let's hear it now.'

Again she hesitated. 'I was sent to test my skills to the full and to – and to - .'

'And to what?' I demanded.

'To see if I could sense the presence of any advanced life forms still existing on Xenonia,' she answered. 'It is considered that Orion and the bots you carry might not achieve this so easily because they are attuned only to humans and to each other even though they are intelligent in a different way.'

Her answer surprised Karin and myself, of course, and needless to say we found it altogether fascinating. If we encountered any self-aware life form it would have to be very different than ourselves.

'Now hold on, Melina,' I responded, 'so you're at least *that* good are you? Does that mean none of us are safe from being probed from inside that head of yours if and whenever you consider it necessary?'

'No, Brett, it is not like that! It is true I sense superficialities with ease but I will not go beyond that. It is not my remit to intercept other people's thoughts unless - unless there is possible danger arisen. Such discretion was instilled into me from the very beginning.'

'So you don't sense any danger right now,' I said.

'I sense deceit but not yet danger.'

'How many others are there like you?' Karin asked.

'A small number; perhaps ten or so. The Europeans began work in secret several years ago on the project that resulted in such as myself.'

'And is Franz Bergmann aware of your abilities?' I asked.

'No he is not. The man whose place he took was fully aware but said nothing to him – through resentment I believe. Few people know of us outside our research facility although others must have guessed and there are certainly rumours. It is now I feel circumstances demand I speak out. I will trust to your understanding and to your discretion.'

'You can rely upon us for that,' Karin assured her, glancing aside at me.

'Yes you can,' I agreed, 'except that sooner or later it may become obvious may it not, especially if you...'

'As you say, Brett, sooner or later it may become obvious.'

'Well I'll soon be having a word with our friend Bergmann because there's something I was informed about only minutes before meeting up with you two that I reckon will connect with whatever you feel is on his mind.'

I imparted to them the information I'd received from Amalia then called upon Orion to lock onto and keep track on the vessel following us as soon as it came within her range. That, I figured would be during our deceleration phase when approaching Xenonia. I left Karin and Melina alone to discuss matters and stepped along to the quarters occupied by Franz Bergmann. We were hardly on our way and already problems were arising. While assuming his door would be unlocked, I nevertheless tapped through a consideration of good manners I hardly entertained right then. 'Yes!' I heard him call so I pushed open the door to find him rising from the bed where his crew suit top lay most carefully and neatly folded on the lower end.

'Finished with Bach have you, Franz?' I asked as he stood before me in shirt and trousers.

'I was simply resting, Commander; what is it you need to discuss that warrants invasion of my privacy?'

'Shall we sit?' I responded, easing aside for my own use the only seat in there. Franz reached to pull on his crew suit top, sat down on his bed and continued to stare at me hard-faced as I spoke. 'Now tell me, Franz, I'm informed your professional status was supposed to cover hyperdrives but how and why did you jump in at the last minute before leaving Earth with Melina and Bernard? Exactly *who* are you working for and how come we're being tailed by a vessel from Earth I'm sure you know all about when there were supposed to be only three hyperdrives available at the time we set off?'

'Oh, so they have launched the shuttle already have they,' he breathed.

'It would seem so,' I responded, suspecting that he already knew they had, 'and Orion right now is tracking her. Please go on.'

'Commander Anderson, the vehicle following us will present no danger to your side of the operations. It contains more bots and support equipment that it was not convenient for me to have aboard the cargo ship. It represents the new co-operative alliance between Europe and the United American States to ensure their involvement here with the latest technology before other powers on Earth catch up. Combining our resources will therefore be an advantage to both parties. We are aware of course that this Planet X - Xenonia as you are pleased to call it, will not remain for long in its present orbit. Going there, however, also confirms the potential for exploitation of the Kuiper Belt and our own outer planetary moons. This they see as offering huge potential.'

'And your role in all of this?'

'I was go-between for both parties and travelled physically between them so as to maintain total secrecy of information. That and my close involvement with hyperdrive technology was the reason for my nomination. Yes, I helped negotiate the agreement and they had me join this expedition to ensure our mutual programme was carried out in full.'

'Aren't you forgetting something, Franz?' I queried.

'What are you suggesting?'

'I'm not suggesting, Franz, I'm reminding you; this whole operation was initiated by Joe van Allen, our president on Mars. It was *our* observatory discovered Xenonia and with Orion *we*, that is myself and Karin as heads of the small team, pioneered the first human voyage beyond Mars orbit when we dropped by to explore Titan. Our original agreement for this latest expedition was with Europe *only*. The fact that other arrangements have now been made back on Earth with Mars' involvement treated almost as a sideline is of no consequence to me.'

I thought for a moment he was going to lose his temper but he took a deep breath, gazed momentarily at the backs of his hands and said, 'And may I remind *you*, Commander, that the UAS owned this vessel you saw fit to abscond with on your return from Titan. Also, once in orbit about

Xenonia, the service vessel will be *my* concern. I will have an automated programme to follow that can be fully implemented once the shuttle has arrived.'

'The UAS,' I responded, 'had too many problems at the time to worry about Orion but in any case we *earned* possession of her. And yes, you will be largely responsible for the service vessel once we're in orbit but I also have a programme that covers responsibility for Orion and all onboard and that includes you, Franz, as well as Melina and Bernard. Whatever is carried by that ship following us you refer to as a shuttle I will *not* allow to compromise our operation!' With that I got up and left him to think over our encounter while I set off to update the rest of our crew on the control deck.

I joined the other four to find the movie suspended and the viewing space ahead occupied by gently flowing cloudlike images intended to bestow a sense of peace and tranquillity. Having discussed matters with them it was agreed nothing was to be done for the time being or until we reached Xenonia so after some further deliberation Sunita, Bernard and Melina decided to continue with the interrupted movie and I, followed by Karin, set off once more to the gymnasium.

An hour later, back in our quarters we freshened up and made our way back to the control deck where we found Franz had joined Bernard, Sunita and Melina in our small group of seats from where all, with cups of coffee, were drifting through some of Earth's greener landscapes on the main display with accompanying music. A journey of nostalgia, it seemed. We got a nod from everyone, even Franz. Once again it struck me how bizarre a situation this was – a group of cosseted people indulging in pretty mundane entertainment while hurtling through deep space at a hitherto unimaginable speed. It might almost have been a near Earth or around the Moon tourist outing. Another thought crossed my mind; I once heard it said that the journey could be more gratifying than the destination and I wondered how true that might be on this occasion. Other time-passing diversions followed though after a while Franz left our small group without offering any acknowledgement. Karin and I were continuing to relax when through our earlobes came a message from Orion to say that the pursuing vehicle was closer to us but now maintaining its distance. Next followed a reminder to say we were twelve hours out from Mars and might wish to take our first rest period. This latter communication had been received and accepted by everyone present so we switched off the Earthscapes and had the stars ahead of us reappear.

After this, the following wakeful hours on board Orion, mainly up front or in the dining area, passed without anything of real significance other than speculation about the obvious, our ultimate destination and what might be found there. Except for Franz, whose comments were few and far between. Karin and I, joined a short time later by Sunita, took further advantage of the gym. After half an hour of none too vigorous exercises we left

Sunita, intent upon completing her yoga exercises, which we felt she preferred to do alone. We rejoined the rest of our crew on the control deck with seats swivelled into position for easier conversation but after ten or so minutes Franz upped and left us. No one commented upon this although Melina turned to watch him depart as if a question remained unanswered. 'I have tried to ignore him these last few hours,' she said at last, 'though just now I allowed myself to sense his thoughts.'

'And your conclusions?' I asked as she arose to leave.

'I have found his aura confusing and not altogether pleasant and right now I do not trust him.'

'Hardly surprising,' I muttered as she departed the control deck. I might have followed her but was at that point distracted by Bernard who drew my attention to more status information scrolling up on our main display.

In the gymnasium, Sunita was preparing to leave when the door slid aside and Franz Bergmann entered, closing the door behind him. They stood facing each other for some moments then Sunita took a deep breath and asked, 'What do you want, Franz? I am on my way out.'

Standing close between herself and the door he replied, 'Sunita, I think we should come to an understanding. Join me when I return to Earth. We could work together as we once did. I do have feelings you know.'

'Well I cannot say *I* ever noticed them, Franz, so you continue with your life back on Earth and I will continue with mine on Mars where I am perfectly happy. I must go now if you will let me by.'

Bergmann, his eyes fixed hard upon her, his breath touching her face as a spectral hand, did not move aside but declared, 'Look, Sunita, whatever we gain from this voyage will in the end have little to do with Joe van Allen's petty kingdom on Mars. Join me and I can offer you more than you will ever achieve there. You will see I am right.'

Sunita, feeling rightly intimidated, tried to move aside then pulled back as he reached suddenly to grasp her shoulder. At that moment the door reopened and Melina appeared. 'Sunita,' she said as Franz lowered his arm, 'we are waiting for you. Will you come now?'

Bergmann seemed about to speak but backed aside and said nothing more as Sunita pushed by and left the room with Melina. They proceeded to Sunita's quarters where they stood face to face and Melina said to her, 'I know he is obsessed by you and I well understand you find him most disagreeable. He has plans that are not in our interest but these still are still fermenting within his mind. We must speak to Brett and Karin about this.'

'No,' replied Sunita, 'I have no wish to make matters worse.'

'I believe matters will become worse if we do not speak at least with Brett,' she responded.

Once Karin and I were informed of this episode by both of them, at Melina's insistence, I was inclined to challenge the guy over his behaviour and his intentions. Karin, however, thought it was in the interest of us all to remain a cohesive team for as long as possible under the circumstances. I reluctantly agreed, for the time being, not to set off looking for Bergmann. Melina's ability to sense what people had in mind was proving quite an asset. You may recall my asking Orion to keep a closer eye on Bergmann, which she did, but without realising the importance of this episode. I next, however, ordered Orion to follow him always when out of my sight and alert me at once should he approach Sunita when no one else was present. If he caused further problems I would take over his entire operation whether we could make use of it or not.

The next rest period was taken with enthusiasm by Sunita and Bernard, both of whom wished to engage in extended dream fantasies. Whether separately or together in his or her quarters I considered none of my or anyone else's business. Melina must have noticed also but made no comment. When eventually gathered together for entertainment or meals, conversation proceeded amiably enough though Sunita avoided sitting close to or conversing at any length with Franz while making it obvious she desired the company of Bernard as he did hers. I avoided further mention of the space vehicle following us whilst listening to Franz explain somewhat dryly how it was really Earth taking the lead in this venture. 'Without the hyperdrives,' he informed us once more, 'the exploration and exploitation of Titan's resources would not have been possible and we, of course, would not be sitting here to discuss it.'

Karin offered him a challenging stare. Except for a nonchalant shrug, I ignored the man as did the others.

Then the final rest period. In the privacy of our quarters, Karin and I lay together to share our dreaming as we often did, once more on this occasion to revive memories of our adventure of a few short years ago on Mars; an adventure most precious that would live with us through the rest of our lives. In this dream we walked one morning through the red desert to approach on foot the rising precipice of a remote and formidable mesa. There we again passed through that sinister dark and ever narrowing gallery within the mesa to at last enter, hand in hand, a strange and secret sheer-walled box canyon, a sunlit place that we crossed in reverence. There at the far side we found before us, set atop a clustered gathering of stone pillars, crystals that sang out in wondrous colour and sound as light from the rising sun began to fall upon them. And because this was but a dream we were without pressure suits so we could laugh aloud together and bathe in the glory of this radiant and marvellous spectacle.

'How many times?' Karin sighed when we awoke. 'How many times?'

'I haven't been counting,' was my reply. 'Each time seems like it's the very first.'

'Yes,' she smiled, 'each time like the very first.'

'And *this* is our last rest period before we reach Xenonia,' I announced, rising from the bed. 'Let's get showered and into breakfast before the fun begins.'

'Fun, Brett?' she grinned. 'I'm not too sure about that.'

'Well alright, but what ever happens we'll still be making history just by showing up.'

My comment was duly followed by the voice of Orion directly to our ears, 'Brett, Karin, deceleration will begin in two hours as scheduled.'

Breakfast was a relatively quiet affair with all our thoughts, so I imagined, set upon the same thing. Seated a short time later on the control deck the six of us gazed ahead into star-strewn space with conversation passing about in little more than a whisper, eyes switching aside frequently to the information read-out at one side of the main display where speed and distance were indicated. Franz Bergmann watched the readout with unwavering interest but without comment.

'Deceleration will commence in fifteen minutes,' announced Orion at last.

What we had regarded as a cosy ride was almost over. Reality was beginning to assert. Deceleration would last for around one hour, though we would feel nothing at all other than apprehension. Low level conversation resumed although Melina remained deep in thought with her eyes half closed. My thoughts returned to the unmanned vehicle trailing us. This would catch up as we slowed to approach our destination.

We had crossed the eccentric orbit of Pluto and travelled immensely further across and above the Kuiper Belt, that vast circle of boulder rubble, mainly ice and rock, in solar orbit and beginning just beyond the orbit of Neptune. Although these possible obstacles in the Kuiper were separated mainly by vast distances, Orion would proceed with due caution as we descended. All six of us were seated in an atmosphere of expectation when Orion stated, 'We will achieve Xenonia orbit in one hour where I will establish the agreed altitude of five hundred kilometres. There our three vessels will be able to dissemble for independent operation. I have detected eight significantly large objects in orbit about the planet. These I interpret as captured members of the Kuiper Belt rather than original moons. Anything small enough I will eliminate should it pose a threat, otherwise space about Xenonia is clear and safe for planned operations.'

'I take it then we are very soon to observe the planet,' said Franz.

'Not so,' Bernard responded, 'there's no sun to illuminate it is there so the thing will be in near total darkness.'

'When the time is right,' I informed them, 'we'll release and activate our Apollo satellites in a lower orbit and have Orion synchronise with them from close behind.'

'It could be the first real light this world has experienced in an unimaginable passing of time,' said Karin, 'I cannot wait to see what lies below.'

'I wonder,' said Sunita, 'if we will find any surface evidence that life once existed there.'

'Maybe a *Keep Outta Here* notice,' I put in. Karin dug me in the ribs. Melina smiled.

We all gazed ahead into space expecting to see what – to see anything there might be, when Orion announced, 'We will achieve Xenonia orbit in thirty minutes.' We gazed harder but all we saw, as before, were the stars. That we had slowed drastically and were still decelerating was evident from the information display but when Orion reported, 'We will achieve Xenonia orbit in fifteen minutes,' something strange was happening.

'Ah, look!' cried Sunita, gesturing at the view ahead of us.

'Yes-oh-yes!' Bernard exclaimed, part rising from his seat.

As we stared we realised we were observing an area where there were no stars visible. Instead, a shadow form, defined only vaguely by starlight, was resolving and growing larger as we approached.

'I guess this is it, folks,' I announced as the rogue planet began to obliterate our view of the starry heavens.

'Brett,' said Karin, leaning forward and pointing to the image area, 'look hard - d'you see anything on the surface?'

I stared then I answered, 'Yes, sure I do – lights, maybe fires. Volcanoes I take it.'

'Yes, that's what they are. There *is* volcanic activity as we were sure we'd detected from the observatory.'

'So in a way there is *something* alive down there,' Sunita breathed.

Chapter 4 - Xenonia

We were standing, peering intently as the dark form grew to dominate most of our viewing area.

'We are now entering predetermined orbit,' announced Orion.

'This is truly wonderful,' said Melina, softly.

'Can you improve the image?' I asked Orion.

'Yes, in different wavebands with enhanced colours but you will gain more detail over features lower down with the Apollo satellites. I will also undertake a more intensive scan to better determine the physical nature of the planetary surface and what lies below it,' then she added, 'The pursuit vehicle sent out from Earth is ten kilometres distance and about to enter our orbit. She will join with us in approximately eighteen minutes.'

I glanced aside to see Franz Bergmann looking smug as he folded his arms in a gesture of satisfaction. I intended to question him further about what was actually in the thing now it was closing on us but for the time being, I had Orion set at an hour and thirty minutes for one circuit of Xenonia with our entire group of vessels, pretty certain his follow-up ship would keep its distance, which it did.

Our tense silence was interspaced from time to time with hushed conversation as we stared intently at this new revelation. As we passed around the planet, the surface of Xenonia was showing broad though often confusing detail. Jagged mountain ranges were obvious enough and deep valleys, many areas coated with white ice, water frozen steel-hard. Visible also was the occasional fiery glare that further emphasised volcanic activity. From some of the volcanoes emerged vast clouds of ash or dust that drifted and spread in the nitrogen atmosphere. After our preliminary orbit Karin said, 'Well I think we've all looked hard enough but I for one could see no artificial structure of any kind and nor has Orion or she would have informed us.'

'No,' agreed Bernard, 'there are no roads, no remains of cities, nothing at all to indicate the one time presence of life, intelligent or otherwise.'

'When we go down there to take a closer look,' said Sunita, 'we will learn more.'

'The ground vehicle or either of our skimmers will be ideal for close contact,' I said.

'We have an entire planet big as Earth to explore,' added Karin. 'We'll need to choose carefully what we want to look at in the time we have.'

That was so. We had no firmly agreed time schedule to comply with as we had little idea as to what we'd be facing but I figured up to eight days might see us through provided we made good use of the bots.

'I have identified an initial number of areas beneath the surface where voids exist,' announced Orion. 'Some of these you may consider worthy of investigation. Precise navigational information will be available as required.'

The display was showing a colour-coded representation of Xenonia as we passed above with

Jeffrey Peter Clarke

next to it a key to the colours. These indicated altitudes above mean level but of greater interest to us were the subsurface voids. During this time, Melina had said very little but her attention was set upon Franz when he turned to me, saying, 'Meanwhile, Commander, how long before you allow separation of our vessels so that I may take rightful control of that assigned to myself?'

'Very soon, Franz,' I responded, 'not forgetting that, if necessary, the food processing section is to be shared with all of us as agreed between Mars and Earth.' It had already occurred to me that the laboratory, allocated wholly to him, might be something more than that. Although the person he had replaced would most likely have been a scientist like Karin, Bernard or Sunita, Franz Bergmann was hardly a lab man. No, he may have been a top hyperdrive specialist but as I saw it he was also a company man intent upon seeing the powers on Earth gain prestige through his efforts and whatever came after it, as well as anything he'd been promised. He'd also mentioned having an automated programme to follow and now seemed a good time for me to find out more. I turned to him, saying, 'Okay Franz, it may not be under my jurisdiction but before we go any further I have to know more than you've already told me and exactly what that pursuit vehicle you have hanging around out there contains.'

He looked at me for dubious moments then replied, 'The four large bots, helibots, are intended to reach the planet's surface under their own power and to identify likely areas for further investigation. They will obtain information as well as samples. They will analyse these in my laboratory and return them to the shuttle. This will then proceed independently back to Earth. Have I answered your question?'

'Not much hard work in any of this for you is there, Franz, so I guess you won't be joining us down there. And I don't want that vessel of yours setting off from orbit before Orion – d'you read me?'

'As you wish, Commander.'

Melina, watching him from behind, glanced knowingly at me even before he'd finished speaking. Her expression was more than that for through it I could almost hear her unspoken words. It informed me that Bergmann was not telling the whole truth but by then something else was waiting to be done. I placed my index finger to my left ear and said in a low voice, 'Orion, initiate primary orbital separation procedure and give us full visual coverage of this happening.'

As we sat down to wait, Franz strode purposefully away without another word, briefcase in hand.

'I wonder where he's off to,' I muttered.

On hearing me, Bernard responded with a shrug and, 'No idea unless it's to what he sees as his own territory. But he'll have to rejoin us at some point, I would have thought.'

'He intends to deceive you very soon,' breathed Melina, leaning towards me. I might have hurried off after him but now the time was approaching to watch our three units separate.

We all, except perhaps for Melina, were wondering why Bergmann had chosen not to witness the forthcoming event. Orion was putting out three Apollo satellites to circle about within her control field so we'd have a grand view of what was going on out there. A few seconds passed then on the display ahead of us, against the blackness of space, appeared our illuminated fleet. After a few minutes what we awaited was still not happening then, 'There will be a short delay in separating,' announced Orion, 'until Franz Bergmann has completed his passage through the airlock and into the service vessel.'

'Orion,' I asked, 'what's he taken with him in that briefcase?' It seemed right then of some importance that I knew what he carried.'

'The briefcase is screened to prevent examination of its contents.' There came a short hesitation then Orion confirmed, 'The airlock is closed and sealed. Franz Bergmann has entered the service vessel. Am I to continue?'

'Yes, continue,' I answered, regretting then that I had not prevented Bergmann leaving.

'This is ridiculous,' declared Bernard, 'He's been ignoring Melina and myself when this was planned as a co-operative affair from the beginning.'

There was no response to his comment because our attention was elsewhere. We watched while, slowly, the service vessel began to separate from us.

As she drifted clear and stabilised her position some twenty metres away, the cargo ship was moving aside to occupy a minimal distance from us where she'd be close enough to join with Orion via the flexible airlock. Remaining under the control of myself or Karin, through Orion, the cargo vessel would, when needed, drop us down into the lower atmosphere where would be deployed one of our helicopter skimmers. Keeping her under direct control of the mother ship was intended also to prevent any possible interference by Bergmann. Being free of the hyperdrives carried from Earth and occupied now mainly by the skimmers, the cargo ship might eventually be used to transport in sealed containers anything large we cared to carry back from Xenonia to Mars. I imagined Franz Bergmann might have had similar ideas.

When pre-planned orbital deployment was completed my attention was once again on Bergmann. I decided to contact him and find out what he was up to but something else was happening outside. The shuttle, the intruder vehicle sent out from Earth was closing on the service vessel. Turning slowly it appeared about to establish physical contact with the laboratory section.

'Brett, what *is* he up to?' Karin asked.

'He's made clear some of it,' I replied. 'But you, Bernard, and you, Melina; you came over to Mars with him as his team; have either of you wondered why he's cutting you both out of the act?'

'No, Brett,' replied Bernard, 'but like I say, Melina and I *were* supposed to be working with him though it no longer seems that way.'

'He has deceived us all,' said Melina. 'I should have foreseen his leaving Orion like this so from now on I will allow more freedom to the abilities I possess.' She looked hard at me then added, 'I believe you, Brett, are already aware of his intentions.'

'Okay,' I responded, 'Bergmann confirmed that the vehicle connecting up with him carries four helibots and maybe other equipment. I reckon what he's really set up for is an *entirely* automated exploration without need of our Apollo satellites. As his bots are helicopters they won't be able to do any more than pick up surface samples so I reckon they'll carry microbots to delve into those regions of Xenonia that Orion has already identified. Any evidence they collect will, as he says, be checked over in that laboratory of his and he won't need to lift a finger or take any risks.'

'Yes,' agreed Sunita, 'and should he find evidence of life there he perhaps will have it on the way back to Earth before we have completed our own investigations, unless you stop him.'

'Hang on there,' put in Bernard, 'we can surely do the same and keep ahead of him - can't we?'

'So we can,' I responded, 'but as we know, the idea of this whole expedition was to ensure human involvement. What're we here for if everything is to be done by robots? We're out in the cold if he succeeds and that includes the two of you who were supposed to be working with him. Bergmann wants to be sole star of the show on behalf of his backers on Earth. Well I didn't come all the way here to see *that* happen! Orion,' I called, 'get Franz Bergmann to show himself. If he's reluctant remind him that he's still within our force field and we can close him down.' I wasn't sure about our ability to do that but I hoped Bergmann wouldn't be either. Within a minute, however, the scene before us faded and Franz Bergmann faced us from where he appeared to be seated in some kind of technically well equipped office. He looked out at us, saying, 'Yes, Commander, you wish to speak with me.' It seemed Orion had not needed to coerce him.

'Franz,' I responded, 'whatever you're up to must in no way compromise our planned programme; that I will not allow.'

'Will you not, Commander - will you not. Well may I remind you this is a separate operation conducted by myself on behalf of interests on Earth.' He peered directly at Sunita, adding, 'Of course, sharing it with you, Sunita, would be an added benefit to us both and I must ask you again to consider joining me.'

I glanced at Sunita and for the first and only time witnessed anger shadow her face. Then she slipped her arm into Bernard's and replied, 'You are a greater fool than I thought, Franz, and...'

'And you've sold myself and Melina out in the bargain!' cut in Bernard.

'We will support Brett in whatever he chooses to do,' said Melina.

'And that'll include a full report to your backers on Earth,' put in Bernard.

'That'll make no difference whatsoever,' I told them. 'I reckon their snouts will all be in the same trough.' Then I turned to Bergmann. 'If you compromise our main operation through those bots you're carrying I'll have Orion terminate them by whatever means!'

'I hear what you say, Commander,' his expression remained aloof as his image faded.

I instructed Orion to do whatever might be needed should Bergmann ignore my warning, as well as maintaining him within our force field for as long as possible. At that point words flashed up to tell us there was a message coming in from Mars. 'Okay Orion,' I responded, 'let's have it.' The welcome face of Joe appeared in smiling contrast to the one we'd just witnessed.

'Hi everyone,' he announced, 'Orion's been keeping me well informed though from now on I'll always be a good few hours behind.' He was as usual in his office with that ancient clock of his ticking away Earth time as he continued, 'I hope you're all in good shape and maybe by now you're planning a first trip down to the surface. It seems that guy Bergmann is little inclined to co-operate with any of you but I'm sure you, Brett, and you, Karin, are keeping an eye on him. I still continue in dialogue with Earth but we've kept it superficial and Bergmann's name hasn't caused any ripples there so far. Maybe it's not what they say so much as what they don't say. I'm twitching to know when you've reached the surface and what you find there and after that comes through from Orion I'll want to see your faces again. That's it for now,' he ended, raising his coffee cup. Joe's message gladdened us all and fuelled our determination to push on.

'Okay,' I said, turning to the others, 'it's about time we did what we came here to do. I suggest in one hour we take a light lunch and while doing so we check out some of those areas designated by Orion. Once we're down there we'll have two of our spiderbots reconnoitre ahead and check out which way it's best to go.'

We sat around the table to eat, the dark expanse of Xenonia rotated ominously on the wall screen close by and decisions were to be made, including the programming in via Orion of our selected destination. A site just north of the equator was decided upon, close to a branch of frozen sea but as it appeared too rocky for use of the ground vehicle held by Orion, one of our two skimmers carried by the cargo ship would be employed. Either could hold only four people so I anticipated some difficulty in deciding who would be left behind. My thoughts were turning to Bernard or Melina until Karin, who I assumed would be most eager to join me, proposed instead that she, as my second in command, ought to remain with Orion. She would oversee the continued surveying of Xenonia and be there to deal with any further developments, including Franz Bergmann. I wasn't too happy with that because I knew what she was giving up but it made sense as we might have been too distracted once down there to get involved with anything happening in orbit. Bernard was as enthusiastic about going as was Sunita and both had made that clear. As Melina had remained quiet I wondered if she might choose to stay and keep Karin company under these most unusual of circumstances, until she said, 'It was intended originally that I, as a life scientist, would be among the first to go down and I still wish to do so if this is acceptable.'

That had me wondering if she'd plumbed my thoughts for of course, it was acceptable. Karin once again insisted the arrangement was okay and if the mother ship put out four communication satellites we could remain in touch when on the surface and she would receive feedback in real time. With that agreed, I and the three eager to accompany me made our way to the exterior suits storage area close by the main airlock where we prepared to leave Orion. We would not need pressure suits but well-insulated, temperature controlled environmental outfits, e-suits, with life support packs. I noted with some amusement how Melina had found it necessary to remove her earrings and, once ready to leave, had placed these into her utility pocket. Passing through the airlock we made our way to the main hold of the cargo ship where stood the two skimmers. 'Orion!' I called, 'confirm I have full communication with you via this vessel and through the number one skimmer we are about to take below orbit.'

'Fully confirmed, Brett,' came her reply in an almost overly appealing voice. 'I will be with you every moment of the way.'

'Sounds like she's joining you on a date,' grinned Bernard through his visor.

'Gets that way sometimes,' I muttered as we slid open the Armaplast side panels and eased ourselves into the skimmer with myself and Melina up front and directly behind us Bernard and Sunita. I guessed they wouldn't mind that arrangement one bit. Melina must have been well aware of the growing bond between them from the beginning though she had said nothing. 'Okay Orion,' I announced, 'we're ready to go.'

The screen lit up in front of me and we had a view of our cargo ship detaching from Orion. Then we were descending. After fifteen minutes our rotor blades began to turn and as they speeded up a section of the cargo ship was sliding open above us. The ship had descended to optimal height and now on full rotor power we were lifting clear into a wide open night of gleaming stars, drifting aside then dropping at a measured rate. A short way above us clustered ten Apollo satellites under the control of Orion via the cargo ship but also linked to our skimmer although these were yet to be switched on. The area we were headed to was in a hilly region where lay a source of heat close to one of those voids earlier identified. Soon we were paused, hovering at a height of two hundred metres with the skimmer awaiting further orders. Well if you know me you'd realise I wasn't going to sit there just giving out verbal instructions. 'Skimmer, I'll take over now,' I said and the control stick slid into position before me. I switched on the Apollos and the barren area below us was flooded with a light it had possibly not seen in millions of years. 'What's the ground we're about to land on made of?' I was about to ask our skimmer but it was Bernard who enlightened us in part when he offered, 'I check out the material below as being basalt covered partly by water ice and frozen methane. Some of the other coating will be complex organic material rained down after molecular modification by cosmic rays in the upper atmosphere.'

'Ah, yes,' I said, smugly, recalling what I had learned from Karin when on Titan, 'Tholins.'

'Ah, so you're quite well informed then,' said Bernard.

It was as well he didn't ask me about anything else of that nature but in case he did I said, 'Okay it's time to take a closer look down there.' From what appeared to be a small chasm, white vapour was emerging. This drifted a short way before turning quickly to what looked like snow or ice shards that swept to the ground some way along. The skimmer informed us the ground was relatively warm down there with an indication of considerable sub-surface water, which accounted for the vapour. 'Show me where it's safe to land,' I ordered her. 'Make it somewhere we can walk around and where there is possible access to whatever was indicated beneath.' Lower still we drifted but the Apollo lights remained above us so we could set down and observe what lay in the area. With a gentle bump we were on the ground and staring out as far as we could see, which with the Apollo lights situated as they were gave us around fifty metres in most directions. As the rotors slowed I turned to the others and announced, 'Welcome to Xenonia!' We peered through the Armaplast and for a time no one spoke. I'd set down in a clearing with angular boulders, large and small, strewn here and there, most part covered with white or brownish frozen material. Beyond our essential oasis of light there was nothing other than total blackness. 'Do you require a spoken analysis of ground materials?' the skimmer asked. This information was scrolling up the screen in front of me and it would be relaying to Orion and so to Karin who, when she checked it out, would understand it more easily than I or probably those with me might. But we wouldn't be the first from Mars or Earth to tread the ground of Xenonia; there were our spiderbots, Freddy and Ginger. They were named, more or less, after a song and dance routine famous on Earth way back in the twentieth century. Naming bots was a tradition, originated on Mars a short while back, to give them an identity when they were working with you. More fun than numbers and the fact that they had personalities of a sort made it seem natural enough. I had the skimmer let them out and we watched the pair, antennae raised as if to attention, scamper around outside to squat before us a couple of metres away dutifully awaiting instructions. They didn't mind the cold. Each had attached to itself three modest sized tubular containers for storing any samples we might wish to take back with us. You will recall that Franz Bergmann had similar ideas for his own bots.

'Well at least we can claim to be first humans here,' announced Bernard after that brief silence.

'Is the air calm?' I asked the skimmer.

'There is a breeze varying around twenty kilometres an hour,' she confirmed.

'What little atmospheric activity there is,' offered Bernard, 'will be generated by the planet's rotation and by volcanic output.'

'Are we to get out now, Brett?' Sunita asked.

'Sure,' I replied, releasing the Armaplast sides to slide back so we could step from the skimmer. 'Anyone up for a picnic?' I asked. I'd been assured, at least, that we were not close to a super-frozen layer of anything that might melt instantly under us due to the vanishingly small leakage of heat from our boots. According to the skimmer the ground temperature where we'd set down was a modest minus one-two-seven. I eased aside from my seat, stepped onto the ground then trod a gravel-crunching pace away from the skimmer. I don't recall hearing how the first guy to step on Earth's moon felt or the first person to set foot on Mars but they at least would have had plenty of natural light to see way beyond where they'd landed. Here, as the others joined me, we stood in a bizarre arena of artificial illumination, four white-clad figures spot-lit in a sunless realm of frozen desolation.

'What a terrible place this is,' I heard Sunita remark under her breath and I guess we knew how she felt. We were all connected by our e-suit radios as well as via real sound so that Orion could pick up our conversations.

'Your physical conditions are optimal,' came her reassuring voice to the four of us as we peered about. Then came Karin, 'Great you're down there but, Brett, please take care – we both know what you're like.'

'Promise to behave,' I answered. We'd chosen this area because there was a void we felt would be reachable through being not too far below the surface. Where the ground arose like a grim wave about to break some twenty metres away, according to my suit rangefinder, there appeared a gap in the surface; possibly a cave of sorts. I sent Freddy and Ginger scampering ahead with their lights on to enter a short way. A couple of minutes later the male voice came back, 'There is a passageway here; are we to investigate further?'

I had just answered, 'No, wait for us,' when there was one hell of a roar from some way over to our right and the ground trembled. We turned to see a large jet of what appeared to be water, glistening in the light of our satellites. It vented high into the air where the breeze caught it, carrying away the upper part that froze at once as it faltered into swirling clouds of ice particles that vanished into the night. 'It's a geyser,' confirmed Bernard. 'In some places water vapour escapes as we saw from above but in other parts it's liquid I'm sure it will sink back down into the depths to re-emerge in a kind of perpetual cycle. Any ammonia content will retard the freezing process.'

We stood to watch, suitably impressed, but the display lasted for little more than three minutes before the column collapsed to vanish gurgling out of sight. 'Fascinating is it not,' observed Sunita. We agreed that it was, then glancing about in case anything like it was to happen again we carried on to where, beneath the looming cliff, our spiderbots waited a short way inside what proved to be a passage of sorts. This was partially blocked by debris fallen from higher up but there was a narrow gap at the left.

'D'you think it a good idea we all go in there together?' Bernard asked.

'Maybe not,' I answered. 'One of the spiders can go ahead but it might be better if the three of you hang around here while I also take a look inside.'

'I would *not* like to hang around here,' Bernard responded, 'I was only thinking of Sunita and...'

'You are not leaving *me* behind!' cut in Sunita. 'If there ever was life on this world, underground is where it would have gone and that is what I intend to find out!'

'I will be with you also,' added Melina. 'I have no desire to remain out here alone.'

'Fine,' I shrugged as we carried on toward the gap which I will admit looked pretty forbidding and no place at all for us poor humans.

Orion cut in next with, 'I recommend you leave subsurface exploration to the bots; the interior may be unsafe.'

Karin would be copied in and no doubt awaited my response which was, 'Okay, we'll watch out.' And so we carried on. 'Looks like there's enough room to push through,' I said, 'but Freddy and Ginger can reconnoitre in case there are problems.' I ordered our two bots to stay ahead of us by around six metres where they would scan and record all about the gallery. Our e-suit microphones we switched off in case the echoing of our voices triggered a rock fall. Now out of touch with Orion we trod behind carefully with our e-suit lights full on, picking out here and there a gleam of quartz on the black rock walls. The gallery descended moderately, rubble-strewn, wide enough in most places but difficult to pass through in others because of rock falls. If you wanted to feel remote and cut off from everything you ever knew, this without a doubt, was the place to be. Our suit readings indicated the air was becoming warmer. At one point I noted it had reached a sizzling minus sixty.

'I'm beginning to wonder,' said Bernard, looking up as we paused, 'if this gallery is altogether natural; I see no reason for its being here. It bends around quite a bit and it certainly isn't a lava tube.'

We'd gone over a kilometre and I was thinking at that point it might not be a good idea to have all four of us go any further. I considered once again having my three companions wait while I carried on alone. I would let the spiderbots go even deeper ahead and send back images to my helmet display. When Ginger's voice announced, 'We have analysed the atmosphere again and its contents indicate a presence of life forms some way ahead,' I drew breath and the four of us stopped dead in our tacks. I looked at Melina and she, anticipating my question, said, 'No, Brett, I sense nothing at all – no emotion, no awareness of self, that is.'

'Freddy, Ginger,' I asked, 'd'you see anything moving or any dangers ahead of us?'

'We perceive no activity and no dangers at present,' came their simultaneous reply as they continued on. Then another message. 'We hear running water and sounds of movement.'

'Sounds of movement!' gasped Bernard. 'Then it has to be..!'

Then from Ginger a message that had us freeze once again. 'There is also light.'

'Brett, we absolutely *must* find out what is down there!' declared Sunita.

'I guess you're right,' I responded. It wasn't a good time to spoil anyone's fun although I did wonder if being armed might be to our advantage. The passage was becoming less steep, walking now easier, though we were gripped in anticipation of what might lie ahead. The temperature, meanwhile, had risen to five degrees above zero with a humidity of almost eighty percent. As we passed around the next curve we stopped again to peer ahead.

'Yes there *is* light!' cried Bernard.

We continued to stare, trying to figure out where the light, greenish in colour, might be coming specifically from. The spiderbots had also stopped and now, turning back on our microphones, we also could hear running water and what I could only describe as clicking sounds. 'Freddy, Ginger,' I called, 'carry on ahead and feed back to us everything you see.' I turned to the others, saying, 'We'd better give them a minute or so to figure out what's going on down there.'

Less than one minute had passed before Ginger reported, 'We have entered a cavern some thirty metres high in places, forty at its widest and over one hundred long to where it changes direction to continue out of sight. The walls are emitting light. There are many living creatures and we detect microorganisms all about. The temperature where we stand is twenty-two degrees Celsius.'

'Living creatures!' exclaimed Sunita. 'That is what she said – living creatures!'

We'd already adjusted our visors to see what the bots were seeing. None of it was easy to make out that way so we decided we'd carry on. 'Freddy, Ginger,' I called, 'stay where you are until we reach you.' We approached, switched off our suit lights and halted by our spiderbots but for a time we could only stand and stare in speechless wonderment at the sight before us with the sound of running water echoing louder still though running water was not visible. The all pervading eerie green light was emitted by sponge-like clusters that covered much of the dark walls two thirds or more as far as the yet darker roof. From there long stalactites hung with water dripping down to a floor that here and there, amidst the rocks, was covered by interconnected areas of murky liquid you wouldn't care to dip your toe in. Among the life-forms that confronted us were creatures that looked somewhat like crabs, some reddish in colour and others dull grey. These clambered about the rocks, hence the clicking sounds, and greenish insect-like creatures circled about with wings fluttering or crawled amidst the wall growths. The pools of water rippled as if disturbed by the movement of life below.

'This could be the very strangest of dreams,' I heard Sunita mutter.

Melina, who stood a short way back from us, said, 'Yes, it is life we see but I repeat, life that is not conscious of its own existence.'

'This is, well, just incredible!' declared Bernard then Sunita added, 'Back on Earth there are many species of fungus that glow as these do – bioluminescence it is called. As on Earth they may feed upon bacteria-like mats or somehow gain nourishment from the rocks. Those arachnid-like creatures must be part of a food chain together with any other creatures or whatever lives in the pools.'

As she spoke we saw one of the red crab-things quit its place on a nearby rock and scramble up in an instant through the fungus growths to grab with its pincers one of the flying creatures that had landed there. The predator at once dropped back to devour its still wriggling victim amidst the rocks.

'Incredible,' repeated Bernard, 'and nothing in here seems to be disturbed by our presence.'

'D'you think,' I asked Sunita, 'if some or most of what we're looking at could be carbon and gene-based as on Earth and other parts of our solar system?'

'Why not,' she replied, 'that basis for life is considered to be common enough throughout the galaxy – perhaps the entire universe. We will find out soon enough.'

'The temperature around here,' said Bernard, 'means there's a connection with the hot spot not so far away; hence the geyser we saw. It's causing water vapour to rise to the ceiling where it cools to drip and form those stalactites. You can just make out where it's coming from if you look along there.' We followed the direction he'd indicated and could see, further down the chamber, a narrow opening from which steam emerged. 'This cavern we're in,' he continued, 'may be part of a larger, deeper system.'

'What lives down here could never approach the surface,' said Sunita. 'Long before they reached the outside world the cold would kill them.'

'Okay,' I said, 'let's have Freddy only head over to the far end and take a closer look; those rocks won't be safe enough for any of us to walk over.' I gave instructions to Freddy who clambered onto the first rock and waved one of his arms, saying, 'I hope this isn't too dangerous; you know how precious we are.'

94

'Yes, precious,' added Ginger, rising abruptly up on four of her eight spider limbs and twitching her antennae to emphasise the point.

'Get on with it,' I responded, 'or I'll have you both recycled! And you, Ginger, take and store a piece of that green stuff off the wall, grab one of those flying things if you can and one of those others we see crawling about if they'll fit into your containers.'

As we watched them go about their tasks Bernard said, 'I see from my readout there's a significant amount of oxygen here, though not quite enough for humans to breathe. If this was more like Earth's atmosphere we could take off our helmets and be the first to taste the air of Xenonia.'

'No thanks,' I remarked, 'my suit readout tells me the air down here must stink,'

'Quite so,' he responded, 'it contains hydrogen sulphide as well as sulphur dioxide, methane and a few other unpleasantries.'

'Great stuff,' I said, turning to Melina. 'How're you feeling about the place?' I asked. She'd said nothing for a while.

'Oh, I think what we have found here is amazing,' she answered, looking aside to me. 'Quite amazing, and we are all trying to make sense of it as we stand here.'

She was right about that but I'd witnessed enough in recent times to prevent myself seeming too overwhelmed.

'I can give some idea as to how old this and the surrounding area is,' said Bernard. Reaching into his utility pocket he produced a scanalyser which he passed across a number of fallen rocks as well as the opening walls of the gallery through which we'd have to return. 'These are igneous rocks as we would expect,' he concluded, 'and they register as almost two billion years old – Earth years that is. But that doesn't tell us for how long this cavern has existed as we presently see it or how long life has thrived here.'

'It would appear to support a stable though limited ecosystem,' put in Sunita. 'Evolution must have brought this about since the planet was thrown out of orbit from its parent star.'

'But Sunita,' I said, 'if Xenonia has other geological features similar to this one, evolution might have taken a different turn altogether in some of them.'

'As you say, Brett, a different turn; perhaps very different, and we are to investigate further, are we not.'

Investigate further, yes, we surely would but right then we'd hang on where we were, recording everything we could, until our bots rejoined us. Switching my suit visor over to what Freddy was seeing, as did the others, revealed how he'd reached the side cavern from which vapour was billowing. He was perched on the edge of an abruptly descending shaft some two metres wide at the bottom of which, illuminated by his lights, water foamed and gushed. 'Don't go any further!' I ordered. 'Grab one or more of those things living in the pools of water on your way back to us.'

'Yes I will,' came his reply.

Our waiting gave Bernard a chance to further reveal his thoughts. 'This cave system,' he began, 'particularly the passageway, I'm not convinced it's entirely natural, even though we're on a different planet.'

'You mean someone or something tunnelled down and excavated this and maybe some other caverns?' I queried. 'It all looks pretty natural to me.'

'Well the cavern probably is,' he responded, 'but I'm making comparisons with geology on Earth and perhaps that's not a good idea, although this world must have been similar in many ways to Earth before fate overtook it.'

That was something else to think about but now our bots were returning. 'Have you collected the samples we wanted?' I asked as they stood to exaggerated attention before us.

'We certainly have,' both replied in unison. 'They are properly sealed and ready to transfer to the laboratory,' added Ginger.

Over three hours had passed since we'd parted from the skimmer so it was time to comply with the schedule we'd outlined to Orion and leave. On re-entering the passage we hesitated to take a long, last look at that incredible place, teeming with sound and life, then began our laborious walk back in relative silence. I wondered for how long such busy life had existed there and for how much longer it might continue. Directly before emerging to the surface and glare of the Apollo lights, we would undergo complete sterilisation of our suits and boots by treating the robots and each other with spray-on chemicals from our back packs. The idea of returning with any microorganisms our spiders or we ourselves might have picked up down there was not an option. We'd also be checked out by the skimmer once inside, by the cargo ship's airlock and by Orion but these would be automatic and predetermined procedures.

Once out in the open I beamed up to Karin all the information we and the bots had recorded. Next we 'coptered back onto the cargo ship and had Orion call in the Apollo satellites before rejoining our main vessel with the sealed in samples gathered by our two spiders. On returning to Orion's control deck attired in our crew suits we concluded, over hot coffee, that we'd made one of the most important discoveries in the history of human exploration. I suggested we all drank to it with something stronger than coffee but Sunita, quite rightly, was anxious to get to our laboratory as soon as possible, with Bernard, Melina and myself in tow, to examine the living treasures we'd collected. These had been transferred directly by Freddy and Ginger to the sealed units in our lab via an external, tube-like airlock designed for the purpose. Once aboard, Orion had set preliminary, automated examinations in progress and these would now be completed. The possibility of Franz Bergmann being in on this did cross my mind but as he'd walked out on us I considered him of little importance for now. Maybe I should have because we'd hardly turned to make our way to the lab when the main display lit up and Orion cut in. 'Franz Bergmann has had his service vessel's hyperdrive combine its force field with that of the small Earth ship. They now equal my own together with that of the cargo vessel so I am no longer able to prevent his leaving our position in orbit unless by destructive force. He is moving away at present; am I to disable his vessels?'

On display before us was the service vessel and the shuttle locked into position with it. They were rising slowly to a higher orbit and would therefore fall behind us. 'Not now,' I replied. 'Can you have one or more of our satellites keep watch on him?'

'Yes, I will ensure this,' replied Orion.

'I wonder why Bergmann's waited until now to remove himself,' remarked Karin.

'Could be,' I said, 'he's hung around to copy over to that lab of his the surveys we made of the planetary surface and those voids so as to save himself the trouble and now, being so close to Orion, he'll have all the information we just sent up. That's something I should have considered.'

'There was no reason to block him out before was there,' said Bernard, 'when everything was supposed to be shared.'

'Well there's reason now isn't there,' I responded, 'because he may intend using that information to further his own ends. Also, knowing as you must the facilities he has over there he'll have his ready-made programme to follow. He could stay put and have his bots go where this decides.'

'And will he not,' asked Sunita, 'intercept our transmissions to Mars?'

'Yes,' I concurred, 'so from now on they'll mostly be scrambled as will any between ourselves, and should he have any of his satellites nosing about to try and pick them up I'll maybe have Orion zap them.'

'But that,' said Karin, 'could sour relations between Mars and Earth.'

'Then perhaps I'll give it more thought,' I responded. The expression on Melina's face as she looked at me said she knew I didn't mean a word of it and she was right. I would give no thought whatsoever to our relationship with Earth under the present circumstances. We had an agreement and their side broke it, or at least Bergmann had, and this I would impart to Joe with my next relay. 'Very well, Sunita,' I said, 'let's get along to the lab.'

Orion's laboratory was somewhat smaller than that in the service ship, the one we'd anticipated we might use, but our own had well proved its worth at Titan and I was confident that under Sunita once more it would do so here at Xenonia.

'Give me five minutes to get the specimens out on display,' she said as we arrived at the small airlock designed to isolate the laboratory. The five minutes threatened to become an infinity but once the time was up we stepped through to where Sunita waited within the dimly illuminated lab. Ranged against one wall stood a group of three cabinets, their interiors in darkness. Each was sealed and protected by Armaplast screens and all were equipped with manipulating devices, probes, read-outs and other remote control or automatic test facilities. Before each unit was a console with controls and glowing indicators.

'I have replicated the atmosphere and temperature in all of these units to match that of the cavern,' Sunita informed us as we stepped across to gather about the first. 'Three examples are ready for inspection with two more on hold.'

In the first cabinet rested an irregular piece of the fungus-like material, bigger than a human hand, that had covered much of the cavern walls. In the unlit cabinet it glowed the same weird green. 'This as you see,' she indicated, 'still exhibits the bioluminescence we saw down there. It appears in some ways to play the role of a fungus although our pre-programmed analysis tells me it is quite different genetically to anything we would find on Earth. Now we are close enough you can see how the filaments covering its surface are moving, which means it may also have trapped small organisms that ventured in there.'

This we stared at with what we felt an appropriate amount of time before we moved to the second specimen where Sunita switched on the internal light. This contained one of the green flying creatures, some twelve or more centimetres long that we thought resembled an insect though seen close up it appeared less so.

'As we see,' began Sunita, 'the body possesses an articulated head with antennae, four compound eyes and insect-like mouth parts but the abdomen is more segmented. The two pairs of wings appear to have much in common with those of a terrestrial dragonfly and the four pairs of legs are hooked, so like a dragonfly it might have captured aerial prey.'

The creature switched its head rapidly about in an inquisitive manner but otherwise remained still.

'Fascinating,' breathed Karin.

This creature, when not flying, would have relied upon its colour to render it less obvious to predators when crawling amongst those wall growths.'

'Didn't stop one of them being grabbed by that crab lookalike did it,' I remarked.

'No, Brett, it did not and it is one of those we are to see next.'

After further observations by Sunita on the creature's physiology we shuffled along to the third enclosure and on came the light.

'Well there's something else I missed,' said Karin.

'Nasty looking thing isn't it,' remarked Bernard.

'Yet still we find it most interesting do we not,' said Melina.

Bernard was right, seen close-up it was as he observed, a nasty looking thing. It was indeed crab-like and kind of disk shaped, deep reddish with a fine white speckle. What I took to be its shell was about fifteen centimetres across with six pairs of slender legs and a pair of what looked like extendable, claw-like pincers. It was the eyes that might give some people the creeps; they looked to me like - like sort of lizard eyes, one close to each side of the shell, peering sometimes together, sometimes independently at each of us in turn and with a hard-looking, serrated mouth twitching beneath. Everything about it said, 'predator,' so I wouldn't have cared to poke my fingers in there.

'I do not have an in depth analysis on any of them yet,' informed Sunita, 'and there are still more specimens from under the water to examine. But the eyes of this one are not compound as are those of arthropods on Earth but appear similar to those of a squid or octopus.'

Karin, leaning forward to take a closer look, lurched suddenly back with a sharp cry as the creature in the tank sprang at her only to strike violently against the Armaplast screen with an unnervingly loud crack. The rest of us stepped away instinctively and I figured that, had it not been contained, the creature would have taken a chunk out of Karin's flesh.

'Oh, I am so sorry,' gasped Sunita, 'I did not expect that; it has hardy moved until now'

'Hope the damned thing gave itself a headache,' I muttered.

We stared in silence, not quite so close as before, to watch the creature circle jerkily about, click-click-clicking, searching, pausing every few seconds or so to smack one or other of its pincers hard against the Armaplast. When it became still

Sunita said, 'After our work is completed I will have the specimens deep frozen and placed in storage. Out of their natural environment all of our examples will of course die so they must be preserved for further analysis on Mars. It is whatever microscopic life these specimens carry on and perhaps within themselves that must also be considered.'

'You mentioned you have other specimens here,' said Karin.

'Yes,' replied Sunita, 'but these are small creatures still sealed inside the water in which they lived. I wish for more time to examine them. There will be many forms of life within those samples of water.'

'And what's more,' I said as Sunita switched off the cabinet lights, 'there's a dinner period creeping up on us.'

'Yes,' smiled Karin, 'let's go and eat before something else tries to attack me. I need a drink and I don't mean coffee.'

On the way to our dining area I remarked, 'There might be a larger version of that crab thing living somewhere else down there so I suggest we or at least I arm myself for the next visit.'

'Whatever might be found elsewhere on Xenonia can hardly be predicted,' said Sunita.

'You after all, Brett,' added Melina, 'encountered on Mars not so long ago, a stranger form of life than ever we might have imagined.'

'Yes I did but it's never bothered us since and it may no longer be there.'

'Carrying weapons,' said Bernard, sitting down beside Sunita, 'means we might offer harm to extraterrestrial life forms and that's prohibited by International Council rulings, Brett, is it not. And Mars is tied in with that agreement.'

'Sure, I'll go with that, Bernard, unless something tries to harm one of us. We after all are extra Xenonian life forms and we also have a right to protection.'

On finishing our food we relaxed and listened to a little music. During that time, however, the subject of Franz Bergmann once more raised its head when Orion announced, 'The shuttle sent out to Franz Bergmann has disconnected from the main ship and ascended to one hundred metres.' A short hesitation was followed by, 'It has released a rotor-bladed helibot. One of our satellites is scanning this and it appears to contain four microbots, all of which may be drones.'

'Well there's a surprise,' I said. 'And its destination?'

'It is in low orbit and still descending but its present trajectory will take it close to or at your previous location on the surface.'

'What the hell d'you think he's up to?' asked Bernard.

'I think he's taking the easy way out to gain more from our efforts,' I replied. 'And with those micros he may add to what we already know.'

'It wouldn't surprise me,' said Karin, 'if Bergmann intends to gather enough to satisfy the prestige of his backers, leave orbit and head back to

Earth with the service vessel while we're at some point on or under the surface of the planet.'

'But what good will that do him?' Bernard asked. 'We'd be on his tail with all the proof and facts of our own.'

'Yes,' agreed Sunita, placing a hand about Bernard's arm, 'the man would be discredited. What is the point of it all.'

'Okay,' I said, 'let's see if we can have another word with him from the control deck. It'll be easier than doing it here.'

All the time, Melina had listened intently and as we prepared to leave she said, 'Perhaps I can help.'

'You can?' I queried. 'How can you help when you're separated from him by empty space – you'd have to be close by, wouldn't you?'

We arose from our seats and she replied, 'If you make the image large I will study his expression, I will look into his eyes and I will listen to his voice as he speaks.'

'Could be worth a try,' I said. 'Let's go.'

We were seated on the control deck when I summoned Orion. 'Orion I wish to speak with Franz Bergmann. Give us normal viewing size for one minute then have his face fill around three quarters of the whole area.'

For some time all we could see ahead of us was the field of stars but when this eventually shimmered Bergmann appeared. He was as before wearing his crew suit and seated in his previous space. 'What is it now?' he asked.

'Franz,' I replied, looking at a man who bore an anxious expression and appeared a little less tidy than when we last saw him, 'it would help if we were given access to the main laboratory facility as per our existing agreement.'

For some moments I thought perhaps he was not going to answer and might shut off communications but then he said, 'I am under no obligation to allow this, Commander, and as I have earlier made clear, my commitment is solely to those on Earth who have provided me with the required facilities.'

As he spoke, Orion closed in on his face. 'So you say,' I continued, hoping to retain his presence a while longer, 'but no such communication has been received by me as head of this expedition. We have a right to that laboratory, which is why it was sent out here, as well as a right, as I'm sure you know, to draw upon the other facilities of your vessel should that prove necessary.'

'Commander,' he responded, 'I am not responsible for any lack of communication between yourself and other parties, and you will recall offering threats to my operation quite recently. This gives me every right to proceed as I am. I believe I have already made my position clear.'

With those words his image vanished and the star field returned. No one spoke until Melina said, 'The message in his eyes and in his voice tells me that although he bears us much ill, he is also afraid.'

'Of what is he afraid?' asked Sunita.

'He no longer possesses the confidence he began with,' she answered. 'He is isolated and much disturbed, yet at the same time he is impatient.'

'Being out there alone might be his main problem,' added Karin.

'And so it might,' I said, 'yet he's surrounded by all the technology anyone could wish for just standing by to take his orders. Still, I reckon the situation's caught up with him. He's never been beyond Earth orbit before and now, having broken with his own team and with ourselves, he realises just where he's ended up and that's as far as anyone ever has been from Earth. As Melina implies, he doesn't have the confidence to go it alone but since the arrival of that shuttle he's committed to delivering the goods.'

'Then he'll have to get a move on, won't he,' said Bernard.

'He already has,' said Karin, 'if those bots he sent down are doing their job.'

'So, Brett,' Bernard asked, 'do we blast them before they dock with his ship?'

'Maybe not because he'll need to take back with him more than the few samples of life we've so far discovered. We should let Bergmann take on board whatever his bots collect down there, which I guess will include much the same as we already have, then take meaningful action.'

'What d'you have in mind?' asked Karin.

'One second,' I replied. 'Orion, you've been monitoring the helibots sent down from Franz

Bergmann's shuttle. If required will you be able to block their reconnecting to the shuttle or to the service vessel if required?'

'That could be possible,' came the answer, 'but the facilities he has may enable him to counter my actions. Direct physical intervention may be the only option.'

'That's something to think on later,' I said.

We spent the next hour speculating over what forms more advanced life might have taken on Xenonia before and since the disaster and how what we'd so far come across indicated at least the possibility of such. At length I concluded, 'For now we ought to look to our next rest period then after that we can talk over the second location we plan to visit.'

Chapter 5 - Domain of Darkness

Before we took to our bed Karin informed me, 'Brett, while the four of you were down there I undertook further research with the help of Orion and we did come across another promising location, this time twelve degrees south of the equator. I utilised the other ten Apollo satellites and although I had to have them operate at a far higher orbit than you were able to use they gave enough light for Orion to further enhance the scene. What I came across most definitely looked odd. I wanted time to think about it rather than raise expectations within the others so maybe before breakfast you could look at what I saw.'

'Why not now while we're alone?' I asked.

She reached to squeeze my arm, kissed me on the cheek and smiled, 'No, not now, let's take our minds off Xenonia and Bergman for a while, shall we, dear.' I needed no encouragement. We wouldn't be doing any more other-worldly searching this side of bedtime.

Some time later, Karin and I shared another dream. We were back on Mars and sitting, as often we had, in sunlight by the biodome fountain surrounded by greenery and life. This, an encapsulated world imposed by humanity upon a cold and hostile red desert, seemed then a paradise awaiting our return.

Later out of bed, showered and wearing our crew suits I revived the conversation of that notional previous evening. 'You said this promising location you came across looked odd. What did you mean by that?'

'Yes, Brett, I've thought about it since and I'm just as certain now we're up and about as I was from the start. You told me there was some doubt over that passage you explored. You said Bernard believed it might be artificial but when the details were beamed up I was not at all convinced. The entrance I've looked at since is located on a steep rise. The opening there *does* appear to be artificial, at least what I could see of it. It is part covered by ejecta from a nearby crater; probably the result of a Kuiper Belt rock strike but I'd say it's most definitely worth looking at though we couldn't detect any gasses that might indicate life. The rise is well away from any frozen sea although not far from it to the east is a ravine containing a frozen river. A few kilometres beyond the rise to the south is a volcanic region that looks to be regularly active with magma bursting out almost continually from a long rift in the ground.'

'Fine, then we can discuss it at greater length over breakfast with the others.'

We'd finished breakfast when on the dining area display Karin called up and zoomed in to her newly revealed location. There was as we saw an opening and at less than thirty metres distance from it lay the modest sized crater. The visible, left side of the opening looked like part of an arch; so much so that we all agreed it *had* to be investigated though as before, the area was too rock-strewn for use of the ground vehicle. I felt Sunita might want to join us and suggested we use the second skimmer, the first being taken down by myself with Bernard and Sunita and the second by Karin with Melina. Sunita this time declined the offer, saying she needed to continue her study of the specimens we'd delivered from our first visit while they were alive, healthy and in one case still kicking.

As we were about to leave the dining area Orion contacted me directly to say, 'I am holding a message for you from Amalia Barbosa at the Isaac Newton space station.'

'Fine,' I replied, 'we'll take it where we are.' The abstract flowing feature on the wall faded and there was Amalia's smiling face. 'Hi everyone – I hope all is going as planned now you're such a long, long way away. I'm keeping in regular touch with Joe which means we'll share with each other our messages to you and your replies to us. Meanwhile we're picking up all the feedback from Orion. Mars presently has one of those annoying planet-wide dust storms which it seems will last another day, otherwise everything is pretty normal down there. Joe will be through to you before long but for now I hope you'll all soon be back with us. Talk again later.'

Her brief message was welcomed but other matters were pressing and we had to get ourselves ready.

Our second trip down to the surface of Xenonia was undertaken in very much the same manner as the first where from the cargo ship we descended through thicker atmosphere by skimmer with a company of ten Apollo satellites circling above for illumination. This time setting down close to our objective was not possible because of surrounding boulder rubble. I'd taken over the controls as I'm often inclined to do and in spite of, 'Landing here is not advisable!' voiced in earnest by the skimmer, we ended up more or less level – okay less level than the skimmer would have allowed. We were also further away than I would have liked with our goal out of sight around a corner where the land jutted out.

'You don't like being ordered around by machines do you,' said Bernard.

'So you've noticed,' grinned Karin. But this was her first visit and she stared about fascinated as I released our two bots. We slid open the Armaplast sides to clamber out and I charged Freddy and Ginger to, 'Find us the easiest route for walking to our pre-designated location.'

'We'll do our best as always,' they replied in unison, waving their antennae in circles, and so we followed between rocks and boulders at an awkward, sometimes stumbling pace with the Apollo lights above. After five or so minutes we turned the corner and the entrance came into sight. In the distance, visible beyond the rise, a shower of sparks arose and fell repeatedly, indicating the volcanic activity that lay some way out there. As we approached, our lights brightened the opening up ahead and it seemed unlikely to me that nature itself could have created such curved geometry, part concealed though it was. Closer still and Bernard announced, 'No doubt about it is there – it might be pretty rough but this is no natural feature.'

Our spiderbots had halted to squat at the entrance and we joined them with heightened enthusiasm to look about and shine our suit lights inside.

'Yes, only an intelligent life form could have built this,' breathed Bernard as we peered further into forbidding depths.

Karin and Bernard pulled out their scanalysers and Bernard, reaching up to pass his across the side of the opening, announced, 'This is a kind of limestone and registers an age of over eighty-eight million Earth years. There must have been substantial seas on this planet for – for maybe as long as there have been on Earth.'

'Same reading here,' said Karin, passing hers over a fallen stone block. 'This entire area must have been rising and perhaps still is with that river below cutting ever deeper as the Colorado River still does within the Grand Canyon back on Earth – until the water here froze up.'

'But the scanalysers,' I pointed out, 'don't tell us how long ago this passageway was cut.'

'No they don't,' agreed Bernard, 'but it doesn't look as though anything living has been around here in a very long time.'

'Then we have to look inside there do we not,' said Melina.

'Okay let's do that,' I said. 'Freddy, Ginger, get ahead of us as you did at the last place we visited and report back as you go.'

They both stirred and rose up to knee-height, our knees that is, and proceeded over the rubble with lights on and antennae twitching.

'We're still precious don't forget,' came back Freddy's voice.

'Precious-precious,' agreed Ginger.

'Getting too damned conceited those two are,' I muttered as we switched on our suit lights and clambered our way through behind them. A short distance inside, with the illumination created by ourselves and our bots it was undeniable, with the rough hewn walls and curved roof, that this tunnel, almost three metres wide and nearly as high, was a product of intelligent beings.

'These marks on the walls,' said Bernard, hesitating to look aside, 'they're obviously made by hacking rather than by some kind of machinery like the way this kind of thing might have been done back on Earth in Victorian times or very much earlier. Maybe on this world whatever they were never progressed as far as the machine age.'

'I wouldn't be too sure about that,' said Karin. 'We've seen hardly anything of Xenonia yet.'

'Whatever, but I wouldn't take bets either way,' I said as we proceeded on, leaving deep footprints in a pale, fine grained sand that in places looked more like dust. Our lights flickered and danced about walls and roof as we recorded our progress. 'And if Xenonia was divided as nations are on Earth then seeing the threat they faced, each nation, if nations are what they had, might have seen fit or been obliged to look after its own interests.'

'A selfish way of thinking,' said Melina. 'But knowing what was to happen perhaps this is understandable.'

'So it's possible,' said Karin, 'there could somewhere else on this world be evidence of a technologically advanced culture we have yet to discover.'

'Maybe,' I said, 'but whoever or whatever excavated this place sure didn't manage it without considerable skill.'

Unlike Karin, I wondered briefly if Bernard might have been right after all about that first passage, it perhaps being a cruder version leading to what was a convenient natural cavern system. This one also continued down through impenetrable blackness with a slow but steadily rising temperature, but no change in atmospheric composition; in other words, nothing to indicate the presence of life ahead. 'How long before our coming,' I mused, 'had it been since light had touched these walls and from what source would that light have been.' This passage continued somewhat freer of rubble but with small rock falls where parts of the roof had broken away. All about us reigned a profound, an oppressive stillness that, when we stopped for a minute or so, threatened to overwhelm our presence. We switched off our radios and instead relied upon the real sound facilities enabled by our e-suits. This added a kind of normality to the passage even though hollow echoes of our voices rattled back and forth from the darkness as if others unseen were mocking our words. It was nevertheless oddly reassuring. Freddy and Ginger would not revert to actual sound as being ahead of us their echoes would be confusing.

'Still no sign of life is there,' remarked Bernard, as we walked on at an easy pace. 'We've already gone further and deeper than where we went before.'

Again we stopped as Bernard pointed to one side, saying, 'There's a change of rock stratum here. Lower down it becomes a kind of sandstone – not the most durable of rocks.'

'There is organic material laying about the floor,' announced Ginger from further along. We paused, stared in silent anticipation then carried on to find what it might mean. Ahead of us, scattered half buried amidst the sand, lay hundreds of blackish oval objects some ten or more centimetres long, others less. 'Ginger, Freddy,' I called, 'both of you try and figure out what those things are!'

We caught up with our bots and stood to watch them examine one each of the objects, then came Freddy's reply, 'We have each scanned two of them. They were once living creatures of arthropod form but long since desiccated and free of microorganisms. They will not remain intact if disturbed.' Hardly had he finished talking when a resounding crash from behind had the four of us spin about in alarm with our lights stabbing back along the passage. Dust was billowing up and as we stared it began spreading toward us, slowly settling until we could make out what had happened. It appeared a number of rocks had fallen from the roof, the largest over half a metre across. Beyond the debris, as the dust cleared, was utter blackness and in between our seemingly intrusive footprints.

'Does anyone get the feeling we shouldn't be here?' asked Bernard, 'it's like this place should never be disturbed.'

'Could not the sound of our voices have caused those rocks to fall?' queried Melina.

'Yes,' agreed Bernard, 'it can happen under certain circumstances on Earth.'

'I reckon that's what did it,' I said, 'but there won't be any problem in our getting out.' I'd noted with considerable relief that the passage was not fully blocked and there would be enough room for us to squeeze back through.

'But we *are* going on aren't we, Brett,' Karin said.

'It might be better if you three make your way back to the skimmer,' I responded. 'There's no point in all of us taking a risk.' Karin and Bernard looked at me in disbelief and Karin said, 'What – now we've come this far!'

Melina appeared unconcerned and Bernard said, 'I'll stick with it.'

They obviously were in no hurry to give up our search.

'Okay,' I said, 'so we go back to communicating by radio only then I'll take a closer look at one of those things the bots were checking out.' Once we found ourselves stepping amongst the said objects I reached to pick one up only to find as I looked at it the thing disintegrated in my gloved hand only to fall through my fingers as black powder. I'd noticed before it did, however, that it appeared to have a number of insect-like legs. Bernard lifted up another of them with the same result. Karin bent to run her scanalyser over three more then informed us, 'I get no precise reading from these other than that they're many hundreds of thousands of years old and possibly a lot more.'

We could not carry on without crushing underfoot some of whatever they had once been. There was no way of avoiding it, and as I pointed out, we wouldn't be hearing any complaints. A few more minutes and with the temperature at fourteen Celsius we saw what looked to be an end to the tunnel. Oddly, less of the decayed creatures were in evidence here. Our two bots had stopped in front of what looked like the entrance to an open space and, raising up on their legs they peered inside. 'We have a large chamber before us,' announced Ginger. 'It contains degraded organic remains and artefacts,' added Freddy. 'There are five passages leading from the chamber but we still detect nothing in the air to indicate the presence of life.'

'Organic remains and artefacts!' I responded, 'Okay, go right in there and wait for us.' We moved on until reaching the bots who stood a short way inside with their own and now our lights flooding a large open chamber with an arched roof and exits both sides as well as directly ahead. Sand and dust covered the floor in here also and to one side a large heap of rubble lay where a section of roof had collapsed. We stood in silence for some time trying to figure out what else we saw spread about the place beneath those unadorned, rough-hewn walls. Some of what lay around could have been what Ginger referred to as organic but we could make no sense of it visually. There appeared close to one wall objects that once might have been wood and metal, structures that long ago had collapsed.

'Part of that could possibly have been a storage unit of some kind,' said Bernard.

About the floor, part buried, lay a number of metal objects all but rusted out of recognition; some, I thought, were maybe once tools. Noting these, Karin said, 'Well there's proof they must have used iron at least.'

'Yes and there had to have been enough oxygen and humidity down here at one time to help everything decay,' added Bernard, peering at his suit read-outs, 'though the air now is totally dry and mainly nitrogen as it is outside.'

Watched by the others I stepped across the area as carefully as I could to take a closer look at the initial object of interest but felt my boots crunch on things hidden by the sand. The object in question might have been a bench or a table because a tilted linear section of it, held up by corroded metal, appeared to be made of wood, or something that looked like it. 'Wood?' I thought, reaching out to touch. 'If so then there were once trees and maybe forests on this stricken world.' I stepped back as the object collapsed into final and total ruin, raising a spectral cloud of dust that drifted slowly down in the still air.

'Brett, be careful!' Karin called.

'I don't suppose anyone's going to miss whatever that was,' I responded as I rejoined them.

'What d'you make of those?' Bernard asked.

What he pointed to were scattered chunks of limestone that on closer inspection seemed to be the remains of smashed statues. What these remains must once have represented was impossible to say and right then there was no way we could gather enough material to take back with us in order to attempt a reconstruction.

'So they carved statues,' I said, glancing at Karin. 'Statues of themselves or of animals, what d'you think?'

'Or maybe some deity or deities they worshipped,' she replied.

'But why smash them up?' queried Bernard, 'And look, there are more remains over in that corner?'

'Okay,' I replied, 'Let's see what's along some of those other passages.' I still pondered over what might be revealed had we the time to attempt reassembling some of those shattered stones. I had Freddy and Ginger continue ahead of us as we explored further forlorn chambers, more passages, yet more open areas with further exits. There lay about almost everywhere heaped organic objects and possible artifacts assaulted and rendered all but incomprehensible by the unrelenting passage of time. And almost everywhere our lights revealed scattered remains of those bug-like things we first encountered on the way down. Some larger organic remnants contained what may have been bone that turned to powder at the slightest touch of a scanalyser. Karin's scanalyser gave conflicting readings but they all ran into immense distances of time. 'There's an abundance of carbon but only isotope twelve,' she informed us, 'and that lasts pretty well forever.'

Some of the passages and areas beyond we couldn't enter because the walls or ceilings had given way and blocked access. The vibration from these falls had reduced almost everything close by to an even more amorphous heap. We had no idea how many and how far these passages and chambers must go because the place seemed an endless maze but I figured they had to have as many walls as they did to support the weight above. In another, larger chamber of smoother, more highly finished walls we discovered more shattered stones that must once have represented a large solid object, an image perhaps of some importance.

'It's been battered to pieces like the others,' I observed. 'I'd give a lot to know why they did that.'

'There must have been a compelling reason,' said Melina. 'Perhaps this statue and others represented deities they had long worshipped so when their world began to die their deities, or gods, were blamed for having forsaken them and so deserved a symbolic death.'

'I'd say they were destroyed towards the very end in an act of desperation,' said Karin, 'otherwise they'd have got rid of the remains and left nothing here at all. Perhaps it happened when food became scarce and irreplaceable.'

'Yes, food,' I said. 'But they must originally have possessed a basic source of food and a way of renewing it for some considerable time.'

'And water,' added Karin. 'But as on Earth, as on maybe any other inhabited world and the first place you visited, they must also have been part of a food chain. What I'm saying is, they surely couldn't have preserved themselves alone.'

'I wonder,' said Bernard, 'if this, being close to a volcanic region, meant they had access to the kind of environment we discovered in that first cavern. If so it must have been on a pretty large scale, or more than one with places where they could obtain or breed enough food. There's still volcanic warmth down here so water must have been gaining access in those earlier times, maybe from melted ice somewhere above, but there's no sign of it now.'

'That,' suggested Karin, 'might have been before the final cold set in.'

Further speculation seemed pointless. We stood undecided, shining our lights into other dark exits from the open area we'd entered.

'Brett, how far d'you want to go?' Karin asked. 'There could be dozens, maybe hundreds more passages and chambers. It has to have been a large community so there will be far too much for us to survey right now.'

'We could have Freddy and Ginger carry on alone could we not,' suggested Bernard.

Freddy and Ginger's antennae twitched at the mention of their names and both raised up on their legs as I replied, 'No, it might take them far too long and achieve nothing except interfere with our schedule. This place could need a prolonged visit and don't forget we have Franz Bergmann hovering out there.'

'And we won't know what he's been up to, if anything, while we're out of contact with Orion,' Karin pointed out.

'Orion has on board two more bots,' I reminded them. 'They could be brought down here and left to carry on exploring the place after we're gone. If we leave two or three satellites in orbit the bots could beam up whatever they discovered once they were above ground and the satellites would relay it to Mars.'

'Then why *not* leave these two?' asked Bernard, gesturing at our accompanying pair.

'Oh, we'd be all alone,' murmured Ginger.

'Abandoned,' added Freddy, 'and what would happen when we needed a recharge?'

I grinned at the two who were peering up at me then said to Bernard, 'Yes, they do have a point and I think your idea might spoil a good relationship. Anyhow, they'll first need to collect a few samples for Sunita.'

Freddy and Ginger could not of course smile but instead sat back and shook their forelegs.

'I've said this before, Brett,' remarked Karin, prodding me lightly as we turned to go, 'You're at times rather sentimental over robots, especially with that pet of yours in the biodome.'

'That pet, as you call it, is *not* a robot even if her genes are artificial.'

Melina chuckled and Karin said, 'Oh alright but she is programmed to behave like one. Come along, dear – let's get out of this place.'

As we retraced our steps I reflected upon Bernard's remark about not belonging where we'd presently ended up. Against my own logic I imagined the walls might possess within them memories of what must, countless ages ago, have been a hive of life. Quite irrationally I wondered if, left alone there for a time to contemplate in total darkness, I might hear their voices.

We discussed how the sheer physical labour in excavating the many passages and unknown numbers of chambers must have been immense by human standards. And how long had it lasted? It will have been too cold on the surface for them ever to return and failing supplies of food and water must eventually, as Karin implied, have reduced their numbers. Had this in the end led to a final, desperate conflict for resources? In my mind stirred thoughts of the ultimate dire ending as they hunted one another down in chilling darkness – cannibalism. With that I said, 'I'm beginning to wonder if those bugs we saw in the tunnel were heading out to locate food when the cold got to them. Which means they might first have finished off the remains of the inhabitants and any food they had left.'

'Sounds dreadful,' Karin remarked.

'Time has no meaning here,' sighed Melina. 'Before we came and after we are gone time will hardly exist.'

'Not if we leave two of our spiders as Brett suggested,' muttered Bernard.

'I'll consider that idea when we've seen more and when were ready to leave Xenonia,' I said.

We continued back the way we'd come with blackness crowding in ominously behind until we reached the first chamber we'd passed through. We were about to leave this when I spotted something subtly different about an entrance over to our left, an entrance we'd previously ignored. There was a kind of low relief abstract carving all around the edge of it that we had failed to notice through our preoccupation with other matters. 'Hang on,' I said, as I stepped across to peer inside. I aimed my suit light into the room and was stunned at what I saw. 'Hey!' I called, 'take a look at this!'

Karin, Bernard, Melina and our robots followed me into the chamber with their lights and we stared in uncomprehending silence until Melina announced in almost a whisper, 'It looks like – it feels like a kind of shrine.'

An intact stone slab over two metres high and almost two wide arose against the wall in front of us. Occupying its upper section was sculpted a raised image we fought to make sense of. It was a circular form with ten sinuous tentacles radiating from it and what I took at first to be a cluster of five bulging eyes grouped close to the top. For a time no one else spoke until Karin said, 'There's no inscription on it and nor was there anything on any of the walls to indicate they had a written language.'

'Should we assume they communicated the way we do?' I queried. 'They were possibly a form of life quite different to anything we know.'

'It represents one of the beings that built this place doesn't it,' said Bernard, and at least that was how we all, in those engrossing minutes considered it.

There was further silence until once more broken by Karin. 'There's no mouth – fine, they might not have had a mouth as we like to think of it so - so I wonder could this instead be a personification of the lost sun preserved for their communal memory. What I mean is it might have been placed here at the very beginning of their retreat from the surface then revered in the hope that one day light would return.'

'So that could be why they never destroyed it,' added Bernard.

'So we're thinking it had some kind of far reaching religious significance are we?' I asked as we recorded the object.

'Perhaps it had,' Karin replied.

'One last hope for an afterlife,' added Melina.

'There can have been little or no scientific progress here,' said Bernard. 'And even had they or some other life form on this planet advanced far enough to conquer space, where could they have gone in a disrupted solar system?'

We continued to stare until Melina announced quietly, 'I feel much pity for whoever or whatever they were. They must have watched that alien star pass across their sky. They must soon have understood; they must have known what eventually was to happen. They will have watched their sun grow almost imperceptibly smaller and the light of day decline as their world cooled and so they worked to preserve their kind. Then in time, over their land, came darkness. Eternal frozen darkness.'

'Was there a last one of them left alive down here, I wonder,' mused Bernard.

'Perhaps there was,' Melina said. 'There has to be a last for everything does there not; ourselves also. A last sight of the sun and stars, a last sight of those we care for and, yes, a last closing of that once familiar door.'

On that less than uplifting note I said, 'Okay, let's get upstairs. As soon as we're out of here I'll have everything beamed up encrypted to Orion so you-know-who can't make any use of it.'

'Wait,' said Melina 'I think we ought to leave behind a token of our presence.'

'Why?' Bernard asked.

'I don't really know why,' she replied, 'but I just do.'

'What can we leave?' I queried. We each delved into our utility pockets.

'I don't have anything other than my scanalyser,' said Bernard, 'and I won't be leaving that.'

'Same here,' added Karin.

I fished around but could find nothing I'd care to part with, either. And that included the one item Bernard in particular would have disapproved of.

'Then I will leave these,' announced Melina. 'I had to remove them before fastening on my helmet so now they can remain as proof of our visit.' She held out her gloved hand to reveal the pair of jewelled earrings I'd first noticed her wearing when she arrived on Mars.

Proof to whom, I wondered as Karin asked her, 'Are they not too valuable to part with?'

'Yes they are valuable but they are a small part of me that I wish to offer.' She bent to place the earrings onto a narrow ledge at the base of the slab, saying quietly, 'There, when the darkness returns they will remain through untold time as a memory of our presence.'

The earrings sparkled in the light of our e-suit lamps, then as we walked away I asked myself if one day they also might end up the last relic of another long-vanished life form. Ourselves.

During our return through the tunnel we deliberated upon the possibility of finding evidence of a more developed civilisation on Xenonia and Bernard said, 'On Earth we once had advanced societies existing at the same time as others less so who benefitted materially from them but still hung onto a medieval way of thinking. Maybe there were once technologically advanced cultures here but with a bigger gap between those who were so advanced and those who were not.'

'Maybe there were,' I responded, 'but on a planet the size of Earth and dead for so long we might be hard put to find it in the time we have. Let's see what more Orion can do.'

With our spiderbots back on board the skimmer we 'coptered up to the cargo ship which in turn transferred us to the warm and welcoming Orion. With all sterilisation measures completed we stepped out in our crew suits to be greeted by a smiling Sunita who informed us, 'I have browsed through many of the images you sent up. Very interesting, I thought, but my presence would have achieved little because it is life I am interested in.'

'There was none down there, for sure,' I responded, 'unless we left a few bugs of our own.'

'I have had feedback on Franz Bergmann through Orion,' said Sunita, 'He has avoided close approach but has still been tracking us from a higher orbit, partly through his own satellites.'

'Okay,' I said, 'as our findings were scrambled he'll maybe think we scored big time and have his own bots go down there. Until then he won't know how far we went below the surface or what we found there and he'll have wasted his time doing so because it's something sensational he's hoping to come across.'

'But surely, Brett,' said Karin, 'with those microbots he now has enough equipment of his own to undertake in depth searches. I mean literally in depth.'

'Maybe he has but our operation was planned all along as a fully integrated system with Orion herself able to probe deep below and to co-ordinate the other vessels in our group as well. Does Bergmann understand priorities as we do? Those bots of his may be programmed but he is supposed to be in charge of them – he's set himself up as decision maker over there but that so-called service ship he's taken over was never designed to interact with humans to the extent Orion does.'

'Maybe this will have him wanting to rejoin us,' remarked Bernard. 'Shall we ask?'

Bernard did have a sense of humour.

A short time later with Karin in our own quarters, I imagined Bergmann's microbots snooping around where we had lately been and I didn't like the idea. And whatever might Bergmann make of it if they came across Melina's earrings? I called up Orion to ask, 'Can you block the entrance to the passage we left when last down on the surface?'

'Do you require this to be temporary or permanent?' she asked.

'Well I – temporary, I guess. Maybe so it could never be got through by our bots.'

'I am looking at an image of the entrance,' she informed me. 'A small projectile strike on the rock face above it will add further rubble to that already present and render the passage inaccessible.'

'Then do it now,' I ordered, thinking to myself, 'Who or what the hell is ever going to find that place again anyway.'

Karin, all the time watching me, nodded her approval and said, 'Yes, Brett, we should keep Bergmann out of there. I know it sounds stupid but I feel he'd somehow desecrate the place,' though that seemed to be something we'd already done.

We'd had our dinner break when the next message arrived from Joe. We viewed it on the control deck from where we could see the complete picture of him sitting in his office.

'Hi all, or most of you,' he smiled. 'The images you sent back from Xenonia with those life forms are quite amazing and have everyone talking about them here and over on Earth. I assume you're all pretty busy and that four of you have been down to the surface again so I guess, at least I hope, there'll be more news on the way to me as you watch this. Meanwhile we intercepted a message sent to Earth by Franz Bergmann, something I find truly incredible under the circumstances. He didn't think to scramble this one or maybe he didn't want to but Mars was in the right position for us to intercept it through our setup on Phobos. He's informed someone unnamed back on Earth that you, Brett, attempted to foul up his part of the operation which is why he decided to part company and go his own way without Bernard and Melina. Now I never took to the guy and I know full well you'd make no decisions that you felt were not justifiable, but I hope whatever is happening will not compromise what you have planned and that with Orion you can do without the facilities Bergmann is presumably holding onto. I've contacted the Europeans and they don't seem to know what is going on whereas the Americans are simply being cagey, so I have a feeling they're not too sure either. What a goddamned fool that man is unless this move was planned from the very beginning, which I somehow doubt, though I may be wrong. So, I'll have to await more news from you and I'm hoping that will clear a few things up. At present we're forecasting another planet-wide dust storm that looks to be worse than the last, so a few ground operations back here will be on hold until it settles down. Right now I'll pass you over to Amalia who is as usual peering down at us from the space station.'

As Joe vanished another even broader smile greeted us with, 'Hello everyone! As Joe says, what you discovered down there on Xenonia is quite amazing and I'm sure there will be more surprises to come.'

To the left behind her we could see a virtual window that had Mars appearing as if the station was not itself a rotating system. The three quarter sunlit disk showed three of the great volcanoes, much of the vast Mariner Valley as well as signs of habitation. Some of the buildings and the biodomes that were a welcoming home to the likes of Karin, Sunita and myself were visible from that height with a few of the biodomes glinting sunlight. The dust storm, it seemed, was yet to arrive.

'I'm aware, too,' Amalia continued, 'of the problems you are experiencing with Franz Bergmann and knowing you, Brett, I'm sure he won't stand in the way for too long, if at all. I intend to drop down to see Joe for a real face to face with coffee and bourbon. As you know he hasn't wanted to go into space for quite some time. I'll leave off now and look forward with Joe to hearing from you again soon.'

As her image was replaced by that of the star field beyond, something occurred to me. 'Hang on here a moment will you,' I said, then took a few steps away from the others. I touched my earlobe and asked quietly, 'Orion, do you hold a record of the results obtained when Joe van Allen had our three new arrivals from Earth scanned?' I didn't want Bernard or Melina to hear me ask that question although she, according to Joe, was probably aware of it. Joe and I had quite reasonably assumed that they would have undergone some compensation for the effects of lower gravity as would everyone else who was to stay any length of time on Mars or in space. That would include also hormone and antibody levels, bone marrow and calcium stability. I recalled Bergmann having trouble with Martian gravity in spite of being prepared for it on the way over from Earth.

'Yes,' came the reply, 'I retain those records.'

'Do they indicate whether or not Franz Bergmann undertook the usual measures for staying away from Earth as did Bernard Campbell and Melina Montaigne?'

'I have no record of this being done,' she replied. Well that was hardly a definite no but Bergmann might have bypassed the regulations through his position of authority. He might not have considered them important right then because his absence from Earth would be temporary with most of his time onboard Orion which, like the service vessel he now occupied, had Mars gravity. But if he was not, like ourselves, protected from cosmic and other forms of radiation I wondered if his judgement might be affected. If so, the man could prove more than a minor liability. Whatever he had in mind, during our own meal and rest periods, Orion would be searching ever deeper beneath Xenonia's surface for anything of interest.

When we lay resting in our quarters with the lights out before sleep I said to Karin, 'I've been thinking about Melina's remarks last time we spoke to Franz Bergmann.'

'And?'

'I think the guy really has spooked out.'

'And if he has, Brett, what d'you propose we do about it?

'Well, I could still have Orion zap that shuttle craft of his or any of his satellites but then we'd have to take responsibility for him and that I have no wish to do since I don't want him back on board Orion until we leave. We can have him think he's getting somewhere but should he make a wrong move, like trying to quit Xenonia before us, Orion is ordered to put a stop to him by whatever means. As long as he doesn't cause any problems our next priority is a third journey to the surface and whatever comes of that.'

'Okay, Brett, let's leave reality behind for a while; Bernard and Sunita may be doing the same thing right now. She tells me she moved into his quarters a while back as I'm sure you know.'

'Yes,' I muttered, 'and I'm glad about that, except when we get back to Mars, Bernard will be returning to Earth. I hope we don't lose Sunita now she's become one of us.'

'I hope so, too,' Karin sighed, squeezing my hand as we prepared to experience another dream together, 'but that's something to worry about later. For now, let's forget about Xenonia and that wretched man on the service vessel. I want to experience the light and warmth of our sun for a while even if it's only an illusion.'

'Anywhere in particular?' I asked, 'Earth or Mars?'

'The park outside Stockholm on a warm, sunny day; the park where I used to play as a kid. You've been there with me before.'

'Of course I have and that's fine by me.' And so that was where our welcome dreaming took us.

Chapter 6 - The Entity

The next message from Joe was waiting for us before breakfast so Karin and I hung on for Sunita, Bernard and Melina before viewing it in the control room.

'Hi everyone,' he greeted, in his usual, welcoming manner although his smile was regulation rather than natural. 'Your second visit beneath that frozen hellhole might not have encountered life but what you discovered was pretty incredible nevertheless and gives some feel as to how long that goddamned planet must have been wandering alone in space. Meanwhile Amalia and I have again been in contact with the European Federation and the UAS. Would it surprise you to know they've been arguing over Bergmann with each suggesting he's been working for one side rather than for the other. It seems some of his subordinates in the UAS may have been conniving with him for purposes yet to be made clear other than sending out that follow-up vessel. The hyperdrive for that was paid for in advance and bought from the Europeans fresh off the shelf, as the old saying goes. It was whisked across the Atlantic and installed while you were preparing to leave Mars. Anyway, things have calmed down and they have reached a common conclusion – Franz Bergmann, using his status, had taken matters into his own hands and they're far from happy about it. But there's even more to this as we only found out a short while before sending this message. The Europeans had planned to relieve Bergmann of his position but that intention was leaked to him before it had been made official. The UAS knew nothing of this and their still regarding him as top man in the project had complicated matters. Both parties now concede that as you, Brett, are on the front line out there you have to act as you see fit but keep a complete record of everything that happens. It sounds to me as if the guy has blown a circuit so I'll await your next message.'

'Blown a circuit!' exclaimed Karin as Joe's image vanished. 'Well there's another old expression but it comes as no surprise.'

'I think not,' agreed Melina.

'Just as well you didn't join him,' said Bernard, turning to Sunita where he reached to squeeze her hand.

'Okay,' I said, 'let's forget about Bergmann for now and see what Orion's come up with that could be worth looking into,' so I called to ask her that very question. We were still facing the main display when the northern hemisphere of Xenonia, in enhanced and artificial colours appeared, with one region in particular highlighted. This proved to be an area around fourteen degrees from the North Pole. Replacing the image of Xenonia with geological diagrams, Orion informed us that, 'This is a deep and complex system of interconnected chambers close to which lies an extensive subterranean lake warmed by heat from the planet's interior. The area is tectonically stable.'

'Sounds interesting,' I remarked.

'*Very* interesting,' said Karin with Bernard and Sunita nodding in agreement.

Melina continued to gaze at the display then added, 'Surely then, there is life. Perhaps abundant life.'

'Gasses entering the atmosphere from beneath that area strongly indicate the presence of complex life forms,' confirmed Orion, 'but I recommend you have our bots enter the area first and release microbots.'

It was the first time since we'd arrived that this had been suggested except in connection with Bergmann. Flying microbots, their seldom used official name being Microdrones, are a kind of winged bot, no larger than a bee, that our spiderbots can be provided with to dispense whenever considered necessary. They are intended to collect information under discreet or risky circumstances then return and impart this to the bots if not directly to ourselves when that is possible.

'Orion,' I asked, 'is this once again a job for one of our skimmers?'

'It is suitable for a skimmer,' she replied, 'but the area is clear enough in one direction by several kilometres for ground vehicle operation.'

This had me thinking. Orion would lower our ground vehicle directly to the surface and with a capacity to carry six this meant that all of us could take the trip. We'd been limited to four on our two previous visits but to take all five? I wasn't sure this was such a good idea. No matter how unlikely, should disaster overtake us the last thing I wanted was to have Orion heading back to Mars devoid of humans – except maybe for Franz Bergmann. How ironic that would be. It was Karin who scuppered my lingering doubts when she said, 'So we don't have to leave anyone behind do we, Brett.'

'Yeah - well,' I replied, somewhat hesitatingly, 'we've seen off two visits without any problems so, sure, we leave no one behind this time around.' The others agreed even though Orion did not.

We finished our food then dispersed to our quarters to sort ourselves out before the descent. Now alone with Karin I rechecked with Orion over her response should any attempt be made by Bergmann to leave Xenonia orbit and move sunward.

'I will have the cargo vessel close to myself to avoid any interference and I will maintain surveillance of Franz Bergmann from synthetic orbit,' she answered, 'and should he attempt departure from Xenonia by shuttle or service vessel I will disable him. He may attempt to follow you by one or more satellites when you descend. If so am I to destroy these?'

'No, let them be.'

'But,' continued Orion, 'I must emphasise my recommendation that not all of you make the next descent.'

'Understood, Orion,' I replied, 'but we still are.' I knew full well that Karin, Sunita, Bernard or Melina would resent being excluded because this, the third object of our hitherto haphazard plans, looked to be an altogether more promising affair.

'But there are two bots you still hold with nothing so far to do,' I said. 'They'll fit into the ground vehicle bay so we'll take them with Freddy and Ginger. If where we're going is as extensive as it appears to be then we may need them.'

'Brett,' Karin asked, 'why allow Bergmann to continue shadowing us?'

'To keep him frustrated; to have him try to find out what we're up to and what he might gain by it, which will be very little as we won't disclose most of our findings to Orion until we get back.'

We, or I at least, never thought Bergmann would attempt to reach the surface of Xenonia, in particular when considering his earlier reservations and his state of mind.

'Brett,' said Karin, 'I take it you'll allocate one of the bots to serve as a go-between so we remain in touch with Orion.'

'Yes; one will go below ground with us to help Freddy and Ginger explore and pick up extra specimens with the other sitting outside the entrance where she'd keep us connected to Orion via the micros.'

'You said, "she." I doubt Orion's spiders will have names assigned to them yet. If not then you can come up with something can't you since they will need identities. You're interested in history so there must be a couple of famous names we can allocate to them.'

'Okay then, well how about – yes, how about, Antony and Cleopatra - Tony and Cleo?'

'Hm, Tony and Cleo,' she replied, 'sounds okay to me.'

When arrangements were concluded with Orion we rejoined the others on the control deck. We were planning to suit up at the cargo bay when to our surprise a request for communication was received by Orion from the service vessel.

'Franz Bergmann wishes to speak with you,' she announced. 'He awaits your permission.'

'Does he now,' I responded. 'Okay, let him through.' There was a tense silence on the control deck as his unsmiling image was displayed before us larger than life. He appeared to have tidied himself up since his previous appearance. 'Well, Franz,' I smiled, 'what's got you out of bed and looking so smart?'

A studied few seconds passed then he replied, 'Commander, in a single-minded yet justifiable pursuit of Earth's interests, I may have overestimated the facilities at my disposal compared with those of your own, to which it was always intended I should be a party. I suggest therefore that we recombine our resources to serve our mutual benefit.'

'You're in big trouble back home, Franz, whether we do or not, you know that don't you - or do you? There are people back on Earth for whom prestige is everything and they don't any longer see you as gaining it for them.'

'I am of course aware there are a number of concerns on the home planet but if I, if we, achieve something positive then those waiting back on Earth will understand my motives were driven by my competitive nature and my monitoring of the uprated hyperdrive system for which I claim prime responsibility.'

'Monitoring the hyperdrives,' muttered Bernard. 'The damn things monitor themselves and he knows it.'

'Does that mean you'll show your face down there with us?' I asked him.

'Indeed it does,' he responded with a faint smile.

'Leave this with me for a few minutes, Franz, while I talk it over with the others.' With that I had Orion close him down.

Barely had the image faded when Melina said, 'Franz Bergmann is lying.'

I needed no convincing and said, 'Maybe he is but I can't see what he has to gain by it.'

'Access to Orion's facilities,' said Bernard, 'and we don't want that, do we.'

'Only what I allow Orion to let him have,' I responded.

'Fine,' said Sunita, 'but why not ignore him and get on with what we have to do? Until now he has made it obvious he never had any intention of going down there so I am greatly surprised.'

'I'm thinking,' I said, 'we could then keep an eye on him in person rather than wondering what he might be up to in the service ship, that's all.'

'Perhaps that's a good thing,' said Karin and after some thought, Bernard and Melina agreed.

'Alright, if we really have to,' breathed Sunita, so I had Orion call him back into view.

'Okay, Franz, you get to rejoin us but let go only one of those helibots you told me you have in the shuttle. I don't want all four flying around or getting in our way. Some of the information we and our own bots gather can be transferred to you and you get whatever your micros pick up plus a share of whatever specimens we collect – do you accept this?'

Bergmann stared hard at me then answered, 'Very well Commander, but as I do not wish to impose myself upon you by use of your ground vehicle I will take the shuttle and have her land close to the point where you disembark. None of my helibots will need to be deployed; I'm sure yours will prove sufficient.'

I considered his words. He was obviously up to something but I nevertheless agreed. I was confident I'd have the means of dealing with any problems including possible threats from whatever might confront us when down there. 'Okay, Franz,' I said, 'you'll see us leaving then you can follow.'

'Your preliminary journey overland' he concluded, 'will give me time to organise myself and that I will soon do.' Then he was gone.

'It'll be a bit difficult if and when he does show up,' said Bernard. 'Two of us for sure won't want to talk to the guy.'

'Not to worry,' smiled Karin, 'Brett and I will deal with him.'

Melina looked at her questioningly, then at me. She said nothing but I knew what was going through her mind.

We made our way in silence, thoughts buzzing, to Orion's cargo bay where before entering we suited up. Inside waited the ground vehicle, complete with all four bots in her storage bay, and as soon as the five of us were seated inside with the doors sealed, the cargo bay air pressure began to drop. The information panel before us indicated that Orion was descending and would within minutes be close to the surface. At two metres above the ground she stopped and the ventral doors were sliding open. The GV was lowered to connect with solid ground and on releasing her Orion said in her engaging voice, 'Do take care, Brett, won't you.'

'Sounds again like she fancies you,' grinned Bernard.

There was light outside but no one spoke as we peered all about. The light, of course, was directed from all twenty of the Apollo satellites and these we could control from within the GV. Orion was lifting clear so now was blocking less of our light and drifting aside until we had optimum view. As planned we were a little short of two kilometres from our destination which would be reached via gently downward sloping, reasonably clear ground. The Apollo lights, set to follow us from above, gave worthwhile all round vision out to almost a kilometre, which lessened beyond that until any details were lost in blackness. This wasn't a trip designed to admire whatever scenery was visible but primarily to ascertain if there existed any evidence of an artificial structure between here and the underground complex we intended to explore. Before moving off I released our four spiderbots, Freddy, Ginger, Tony and Cleo, and had them, antennae wagging, prance in front of us with their own lights on to further enhance in detail our view ahead.

The engine hummed and our tracks were crunching gravel when Karin, peering through the Armaplast said, 'Wouldn't it be amazing if we came across some kind of road, or what was left of it.'

'With speed regulations like they once had on Earth,' I muttered.

There was further silence then Bernard said, 'No, I think the time that's passed here would have wiped any such evidence from the surface long, long ago. But I tell you what, as this place was once Earth-like there will be fossils.'

'I think so, too,' agreed Sunita, 'and many of them, though all we will have to look at on the way is ancient scenery.'

We had plenty of that, yes, black rubble and angular rocks either side, some close by, others more distant. Some areas were coated with a pale frozen organic material and as we passed close to one Bernard asked, 'Brett, can we hold back to have one of our bots scoop a couple of samples from those rocks to our left?'

146

'Sure,' I answered, 'I'll take over manually and have Tony do that.' My driving the ground vehicle hands on brought a smile to Karin's face as it usually did on Mars. We stopped to watch our chosen bot scrape away the required bits and seal them into one of his cylinders then we proceeded on. At one point, looming to our right we found ourselves passing the base of an intimidating cliff that partly blocked our light from above. We checked it out as rising sheer for over a kilometre. We all felt more at ease when at last the precipice curved away and disappeared into eternal night. I glanced aside at Melina to see her dark eyes wide as she gazed steadily out and I wondered if in her mind she was seeing other than what our eyes told us. The hum of our engine varied as we passed, rising and falling, over a series of shallow humps then the ground was descending steeper than before. Glancing at our console told me we were over two thirds way to our goal.

***

He had watched Orion leave orbit and begin her descent to the surface of Xenonia. Having relayed his instructions to the service vessel and to the shuttle he arose from his seat and reached for his briefcase. This he carried to the main airlock where environmental suits waited in the storage compartment. He lifted one of these out but it took him some ten or so minutes to put it on. He had practiced its use since leaving Orion but still he found the task a minor challenge. Assisted by the keen enough mind of the service vessel and

147

therapeutic preparations obtained from her supplies section, Franz Bergmann had done much during his time alone to allay those anxieties his maturing plans had spawned. He now was preparing to do that which, at the beginning of his journey from the home planet, he might never have conceived. Setting the briefcase down he released the locks that had remained secure since his leaving Earth. He reached to take out the moderately heavy object that had lain inside. He gazed at this, weighed and twisted it about in his hand then slipped it carefully into the right side utility pocket of his e-suit. But why had he brought the gun when at the beginning there had been no specific reason? It was habit - the habit of a man who had climbed upon the backs of others, crushing many on his way to the top and leaving enemies in his wake.

Drawing a deep breath, he stepped into the airlock.

**

I steered close around a ridge to our left and with our spiders leading we entered a kind of natural amphitheatre that dipped lower still towards the base of another sharply rising cliff.

'There it is!' cried Bernard.

We were transfixed by what lay directly ahead because the entrance we'd tried to locate from orbit had been entirely hidden by a deep overhang.

'It's pretty impressive isn't it,' breathed Karin.

We all agreed that it was very much so. Revealed by the light from our bots yet concealed from those hovering above was what must once have been a wide, rectangular entrance five or more metres across and maybe up to four metres high. The massive stone lintel that once had defined the top had cracked and slipped part way down but while at an angle it remained supported at one side by partly dislodged blocks that still formed a sufficiently integrated wall. Though part obstructed as had been the earlier galleries we'd explored there was more than enough room through the remaining triangular gap to allow for easy access. We were quite close when something glinted to our right; the shark-like form of Franz Bergmann's shuttle. It approached low beneath the Apollo lights. We stopped the GV and climbed out to see the shuttle swing around then settle a short distance away towards the other side of the amphitheatre where it hovered motionless a metre above the ground. We stood watching for long minutes before we observed the access ramp at its rear drop down.

'So he made it after all,' Karin said. 'That does surprise me.'

The five of us were using radio contact only, preset so Bergmann would be blocked from hearing what was said between us. We would switch over to include him in real sound communications via our suit microphones once he approached close enough.

'Is this the tidy, not going with you because I'm too important Bergmann we thought we knew?' asked Bernard as the white-suited figure lowered a hesitant foot onto frozen black earth.

'It's not the one I knew,' muttered Sunita, 'he never would have done what we are seeing now; he would have had someone else do it.'

'Could there ever have been a stranger rendezvous than this?' Karin asked.

'He will once more deceive you,' Melina reminded me. 'Please be aware.'

'We'll see about that,' I breathed and as Bergmann approached us with cautious steps. 'Nice to see you Franz,' I said in open voice, grinning through my visor, 'been missing our company have you?'

'I felt obliged to redefine my priorities,' he announced, halting before us. 'I trust you will find this arrangement satisfactory.'

While tempted to say, 'I don't give a damn,' I told him instead, 'We're sending three of our spiderbots in there first. A fourth will sit outside to maintain contact with our microbots. They will fly back and forth with information to update Orion so she knows the situation while we're all out of sight.'

'Then you are sure there is life down there,' Bergmann said.

'You know we are if you were picking up some of our earlier transmissions,' said Sunita. 'In any case,' she added, directing her comment to Karin rather than to Franz Bergmann, 'the molecular complexes in the air here strongly confirm it.'

Bergmann offered no response so raising a hand I said, 'Okay, let's get going.' This was intended as a preliminary investigation but the ever widening prospect of what lay ahead sidelined a caution that might otherwise have held firm. I gave my orders to Tony who dutifully positioned himself by squatting a few metres away from that forbidding entrance and clear of the overhang, saying, 'Here I will wait but better not to forget me.' Freddy, Ginger and Cleo next had their orders. They were to enter up to twenty or so metres if possible and relay to us all aspects of the interior so far. I wasn't sure if Bergmann would have the means to receive all or any of this information but I didn't bother to ask. We saw the light from our bots shining from within and adjusting our visors we then had a view, albeit limited, of what they were seeing as well as a radioed feedback. They were inside a large irregular natural gallery some six to eight metres high and roughly similar in width.

'There is course grit and fallen rubble,' informed Freddy, 'but it appears safe to enter this far.'

We readjusted to normal vision and approached to step beneath the sloping lintel where Bernard and Karin hesitated to take scanalyser readings. These we did not address since right then there were other matters to consider. From previous experience we had come to expect evidence of a roof collapse in these so very ancient locations but there appeared enough space to press on without difficulty. I had our three bots scuttle ahead up to fifty metres so we then had to rely entirely on our suit lights. There was noticeably less covering of grit and dust on the floor than we'd encountered elsewhere and Bernard remarked, 'There's no muck to drift in from volcanic activity by the looks of it.'

The gallery was narrowing a little but again, as we expected, it continued to descend. I led the way with the others following. Franz Bergmann was at the rear with utter darkness closing behind. Now came our first surprise since entering: after thirty metres the walls and ceiling had become suddenly regular at a width and height of just under five metres and this without doubt was artificial. Parts of the surface appeared to be a concrete-like reinforcing material that had crumbled away in places to reveal underlying rock. We stopped to assess our surroundings further and Bernard's scanalyser confirmed that the tunnel really had in places been artificially clad. Our thoughts were interrupted when Freddy's voice came on our suit radios, 'Are we to go further along?'

The only light ahead, that carried by the bots, was but dimly seen because the passage curved around to have them out of sight. 'Freddy, Ginger,' I called, 'go on another fifty metres then report back, and Cleo, return to us now.' By that time I thought it appropriate to have Cleo send one of the micros carried by her back to the entrance where it could have her waiting partner, Tony, relay an initial update of our situation to Orion. That done we carried on a half kilometre and more, ever deeper, with Cleo at my side to find the heat and humidity steadily increasing. Then our second surprise. It was Freddy's voice that informed us, 'Where we are stopped the temperature has risen to five degrees Celsius; the gallery has opened out and there is much light ahead of us.'

'Much light he said!' exclaimed Karin.

'Much light,' breathed Sunita. 'It could be more of those wall growths we discovered on our first descent. They may once have been common throughout much of the planet and still exist wherever there is heat and moisture.'

While she was talking I switched my visor over for some moments to see what our spiderbot was seeing. 'Hell, no!' I exclaimed, 'it's nothing like that at all! Let's take a closer look.' With our suit lights and those of Cleo flickering about the walls and our feet treading hard stone we moved on somewhat quicker than we had been. We followed the bend and were approaching the bots when we slowed down. Ahead of us the passage opened as we'd been told it would and there was the source of light. We continued on until reaching the bots where we gathered to stand in silent awe. Parts the entire roof of what proved to be a long, curving chamber were covered ahead of us in groups of large, irregular white-glowing clusters of a material we were not right then able to identify. Still further ahead these groups had increased to a point where they were joining up to flood the area with a mellow all pervasive glow. As we moved on we no longer had to depend upon our own lights nor did the bots need theirs.

'This light surely is not natural,' declared Sunita at last. 'No, look at it – you can see also where parts of that glowing material have fallen away and there is rubble lying beneath.'

'Most fascinating,' remarked Melina. I recall this being her first comment since we'd entered the passage.

'Yes, very interesting,' came the voice of Franz Bergmann. Though conscious of his presence I'd taken little notice of him until then.

'I wonder what's powering all this light,' remarked Karin as we peered about, 'or do I mean *lights*.'

'It's deeper than we've previously been and warm down here,' said Bernard, lifting an arm to check his suit data. 'Maybe heat rising up from the mantle is somehow the prime source of energy, but how is it converted into light? And this light extends some way into the ultra-violet.'

'Only an advanced life-form could be responsible for it,' observed Sunita and that had me, at least, wondering if that life-form might be hanging around somewhere not too far ahead. We and our bots resumed walking so I had Cleo carry further on until out of sight around the next curve of the ever steepening chamber and use her microbots to explore further still. We didn't have long to wait for within a minute she radioed back, 'There is a smaller passage leading off the chamber and much that appears to be plant life lies directly ahead. Shall I transmit images now?'

'No need,' I replied, 'I take it you sense no danger.'

'I sense no danger close by but there is much activity further within. The micros report several wells with deep salt water below and more life beneath this.'

'Yes, the underground lake!' responded Sunita. 'It could be teeming with life!'

I did not want us to hang around trying to figure out small images inside our visors when the reality that beckoned looked to be within easy reach. 'Okay,' I said, 'we're heading to where you are but meanwhile have your micros carry on a half kilometre further. Try to ascertain how far the area goes beyond that then return all images to Tony for transmission to Orion.'

'I understand,' came her voice.

Bernard stabbed a finger at the information readout on his suit sleeve and informed us, 'It's even warmer here now, almost thirty Celsius and there's already over ten percent oxygen in the air.'

We were about to move on again when a hand fell upon my shoulder and I turned to face Melina.

'Brett,' she said, now using only her radio which meant that Franz Bergmann would be excluded from whatever she had to say. 'Yes I sense much life ahead of us. Amidst it I sense fear, anger and a desire to survive but as with the creatures we encountered on our first decent and as with much life on Earth, there is instinct but little intelligence and little awareness of being.' She stepped away to stare along the chamber for some moments before turning sharply to say, 'Brett, there is intelligent life elsewhere and - and it knows we are here!'

'So intelligent life *does* exist!' gasped Sunita.

'Is it hostile?' I asked as Karin, Sunita and Bernard stared hard at Melina.

Bergmann, standing behind them, cut in with, 'What *is* going on? Kindly let me know.' so I said, 'Okay Melina, switch over to real sound so we're all in on it.' I could understand why Melina done what she had but keeping Bergmann out of the conversation seemed just then to be of little importance as he still would have no access to our bots.

'I cannot say – not yet,' Melina responded to my question over hostility. Further seconds passed before she said, 'There is no emotion, there is simply a growing curiosity but it may be some distance from us and I cannot say where.' Another pause then, 'No - wait! It is everywhere, it is all around us and all the time it grows stronger.'

'Then do you now sense any threat?' I asked.

'No, as yet I sense no threat.'

'Then we have to keep going, don't we,' said Karin, opting to disregard Melina's revelations.

'Oh but we *must*!' agreed Sunita, 'can't you hear those sounds? Brett, can we have our bots collect some small living samples – we do not have the means to take or contain anything large, do we?'

'Not right now we don't so it could mean a second visit to grab bigger specimens as well as a chunk of that glowing stuff that's fallen from above – present unseen powers permitting.' I was making light of this most bizarre of situations, yes, but what alternatives did we have? We could get out of there at once in case something took a dislike to us big time, we could stand around waiting for, whatever, or we could press on with what we came there to do in the first place. There was no comment from either of the men who I assumed might be reconsidering their initial enthusiasm but Karin, Sunita and Melina still appeared to have no reservations as they each took a step forwards.

Over our suit microphones as well as in real sound could be heard squeaks and cries not unlike those Karin and I were familiar with often enough in our biodome back on Mars. We walked on in silence, our minds in near turmoil over what Melina had imparted. Directly ahead of us around the curve, where Cleo waited, lay something that looked like a wide strip of mossy ground with beyond it what I could only describe as a kind of stunted forest that consisted of shaggy-looking bushes and other strange growths of varying height and colour that stretched on as far as we could see. Here and there were weird-looking, bright red flowers; no other colours, just red. As we stood watching, small, greenish-coloured or dappled lizard-like animals appeared and vanished back into the foliage and close above fluttered or glided various insect-like and winged mouse-like creatures. All of this was illuminated from above, yet further gaps were evident where smallish, once glowing sections had fallen away. Right then the passage mentioned by Cleo was not foremost in my mind, and neither was Franz Bergmann who had been trailing behind us for much of the way.

'This place could be more extensive by far than our largest biodome back on Mars,' I said.

'That wouldn't surprise me,' responded Bernard, 'and the air is now oxygenated enough for us to comfortably breathe. Anyone care to try it?'

'We definitely must not!' declared Sunita.

'What lives down here can never get to the surface,' said Karin, 'as in that first place we entered, the unbreathable atmosphere and the cold would stop them.'

'But they have the lake or even connections to a small sea, don't they,' responded Bernard. 'I bet many of those lizard things come and go from there - and the roots of those plants must reach down one hell of a way. This area of the planet has to be highly stable.'

With all of that in mind I asked Cleo, 'How far ahead of us is the nearest well?'

'A little under twenty-two metres,' she replied.

'Okay, you stay here and carry on with your micros. You two,' I said, gesturing to Freddy and Ginger, 'set off together and find a safe and easy way for us to reach that well and look out for anything that might be dangerous.'

'At last,' responded Freddy, rising up enthusiastically on his spider legs, 'something useful to do.'

'Something useful to do,' repeated Ginger as each waved its antennae at the other. They moved off causing some of those few creatures nearby to scamper beneath the growth while others regarded them with pop-eyed curiosity before retreating.

Jeffrey Peter Clarke

All the time my thoughts were on the intelligence that Melina assured was watching us. But what form did it take and where was it?

As our bots were moving out of sight we set off to follow, crossing the metres wide mossy edge before we were obliged to trudge over rough ground through vegetation which fortunately was little more than head height or less. Soon the vegetation thinned and we found ourselves before the well. As there wasn't much room for us all to stand around the edge I had our two bots set off to pick up a few smaller specimens and afterwards go back to rejoin Cleo. Shortly after there was a commotion some distance away with a sharp screech. Several insect-like creatures and something that looked like a lizard-skinned bat fled upwards from amidst the vegetation but as we could make nothing of what was going on there we, or I at least, concluded it must be a disturbance created by one of our bots. The well was roughly circular, between three and four or so metres across with a more or less one third section appearing to have been constructed from fitted stones with the rest having long since collapsed into water that rippled darkly some six metres below – a pretty daunting prospect. A number of various sized creatures of lizard or arthropod form were clawing at the sides while scrambling from or descending to the water and Bernard said, 'I guess that's where much of what lives up here and doesn't fly around may obtain its food.'

'Or something else obtains *it*,' responded Sunita. 'Nature will be nature wherever it exists.'

'Except for what Melina sensed a short while back,' I added turning to look at her.

Melina appeared to be concentrating hard then opening her eyes to stare through her visor into mine she said, 'Brett, there is a flesh and blood life-form that is aware of us. It senses - it knows exactly where we are and - and it draws slowly closer so we do not hear it. I believe it may do us harm.'

'Time we pushed off then, don't you think,' said Bernard on hearing her. He stepped back to let me by as I was closest to the well edge.

'We'd better hurry, Brett!' declared Karin and they began to turn away. But I had a feeling that any attempt to retreat from where we were to the coldness of the passage would be of little use. Then Melina confirmed, 'Brett, it is too late.'

With that we all froze. Sunita glanced uneasily at us each in turn, Bernard pulled her close while I slipped a gloved hand into my right side utility pocket to close about the hard metal grip of my pistol. Melina stared anxiously at me and I knew she had me figured out. A cracking and rustling arose suddenly from part way around the well edge to our left then heaving aside the bushes a nightmare spectacle emerged. Sunita cried out, grasped Bernard's arm and both staggered back as did Karin. The hideous thing, for there was no other way could I think of it in those fearful moments, possessed a green-dappled, grey body with spine-bristled back and it stood part raised to well over a metre high upon the rear two of its four thick, long-clawed limbs. There were no shoulders and no neck for the back-sloping head emerged straight from a torso and possessed forward thrust jaws equipped with gleaming white, knife-blade teeth. There were three dark, bulging eyes, speckled yellow, one positioned centre, one each side of the head and both outer ones of this mindless, murderous predator swivelled about to fix hard upon me. One of us was about to die. I raised the pistol and as with a piercing hiss it crouched to spring forward I fired a shot that echoed like rolling thunder, hitting it between the forelimbs and hoping it had a heart or some vital organ situated there. Various flying creatures arose in panic and a frantic scurrying could be heard from amidst the bushes all around and beyond us Momentarily stunned, the beast stopped abruptly three metres from me with claws raised high, then before it could advance to take a lethal swipe I fired again, putting a good old fashioned slug straight into its gaping mouth. It emitted a gargling growl, coughing up a green liquid to spatter the stones between us with some reaching my boots. It tottered, one of its rear limbs dislodging a loose block from the edge of the well. Upper limbs flailing it heeled over and with a piercing shriek it followed the stone block and plunged into the water where it thrashed violently about for several seconds before vanishing beneath the surface. I turned to witness the expressions of horror on Karin, Bernard and Sunita's faces, all looking at me, and one of relief on Melina's.

Shocked by what they had just witnessed no one seemed able to speak.

'Well there's a good start to our visit if ever there was one,' breathed Bernard at last.

'That thing could have killed all of us in turn from the looks of it,' said Karin

'Let's hope there are no more close by,' said Bernard, 'we're too damned obvious standing here.'

I referred to their faces just now, didn't I, but one was missing. 'Where the hell is Bergmann?' I asked, thinking at first he must still be close by then realising he was not as I slipped the pistol back into my pocket.

'I didn't see him go,' replied Bernard as we all peered about.

'Nor me,' said Sunita, 'he might have left us before this happened.'

'Or he may have cleared off *when* it appeared,' added Bernard. But then, I thought, who would notice with that devilish thing glaring at us.

'He is no longer close by,' informed Melina. 'That is all I can say.'

Moments later came a further rustling from the bushes. I was reaching again for my gun when our two bots returned with encapsulated specimens. We were not too concerned at the time to find out what they'd collected. 'There has to be another, longer survey down here,' I said, 'but if it's with bots leading the way I'll have Orion figure out some way to arm them.'

'Arm the bots?' queried Bernard as we turned to go. 'But that might mean a further threat to the life forms that belong here.'

His remark surprised me somewhat, considering the shrieking horror that only minutes before had confronted us. 'I told you a while back,' I responded, 'that I would take precautions against possible danger from aggressive life forms. Dictates from the International Council about alien life or no - they're sitting safe and sound back on Earth in their cosy offices while we're out here risking our guts to the likes of the thing I just plugged. Maybe we'll take one of 'em back with us so they can shake hands with it and say how sorry we are.'

'What happened will be looked at by the IC,' said Karin, 'and I very much doubt anyone is going to argue over what you did.'

'It's blood was green,' informed Sunita, 'green rather than red; not haemoglobin but copper-based haemocyanin like many invertebrates back on Earth.'

I glanced aside at her, muttering, 'Well I never.' I didn't feel this was quite the time for a biology lesson even if Sunita did.

'That creature and others like it will have their place in the scheme of things,' she continued as we stepped onto the mossy edge. 'Pity we couldn't get a tissue sample. It must be the top predator and will keep many of the other species down here under control.'

'I can't imagine it has many friends,' muttered Bernard.

'And think of all those lives we'll have saved by getting rid of that one,' I remarked. 'But for now I'll try to contact our pal Bergmann and find out what he's up to.'

'Why bother,' said Karin, 'if he'd wanted us to know what he was doing I expect he would have told us by now.'

'Maybe you're right,' I conceded. 'I guess we'll find out sooner or later.'

***

Franz Bergmann, a man consumed by dark thoughts, was making his way alone through the passage within his swaying pool of light. Having switched off his suit microphones to be without the disturbingly hollow sound of his own footsteps, he did not hear two gunshots echo by. His radio he also had switched off to prevent his being located or any contact made. The uphill journey he found tedious but eventually there were stars visible ahead because the Apollo lights were switched off until needed. Slipping a gloved hand into his utility pocket he approached the portal through which he had entered on arrival with the others. By the time he stepped beneath the broken lintel the gun was in his hand.

'They'll hear nothing from this distance,' he muttered. 'No one will ever know, will they. Orion is out of sight from here because it and their damned satellites cannot see beneath this overhang.' He took a deep breath and said once more, 'No one will ever know!'

The waiting spiderbot raised up and looked at him, saying, 'I am not permitted to interact with you,' but Bergmann could of course hear nothing. He raised the gun and fired three times, seeing his victim, antennae coiled in, eyes defocused, slump to the ground on sprawling spider legs. Bergmann slipped the pistol back into his pocket, breathed, 'That should do it,' switched on his radio and turned to re-enter the darkness from which he had moments before emerged.

***

Never having learned how far this bizarre realm extended, we were heading away from the outer edge when

I asked Melina, 'The intelligence you picked up – is it still with us and have you managed to figure out exactly what it is?'

'Yes, it remains with us and ever questioning yet still I cannot say what form it takes.' She gestured across to the small passage we'd walked by on the way down, saying, 'Brett, that which studies us – I believe it is to be found through there. Are we to enter?'

We gathered close to the entrance and stared into darkness. 'Maybe we should,' I answered after some hesitation. 'If there's intelligence maybe we'll find out what it is and how it operates.' I turned to the bots, saying, 'You three keep watch out here and you, Cleo, send your micros up to the entrance where Tony waits. Have them download all our information to Tony so he can beam it up to Orion.'

The three raised from the ground and shook their antennae in acknowledgement.

We entered the passage in silence with our own lights becoming the only source of illumination. The walls consisted of dressed stone that at some time in the distant past had been carefully fitted, but now were a victim of uncaring ages with subtle ground movements having created a number of cracks and dislocations. I shifted a thin layer of fine dust aside with my boot to reveal smooth flagstones. Our suit read-outs indicated a step by step lessening of temperature. After some twelve metres we came to an abrupt left turn that took us into a much shorter corridor where the temperature had by then dropped to minus eight. At the end of this we observed a blank wall on which could be seen vaguely shifting blue lights. Whatever originated these lights was hidden behind another sharp turn, this time to our right. But as we approached the end something was happening - something quite unnerving in this strangest of worlds. We were no longer able to move forward. It felt as if we were being pushed back by an invisible hand. 'This is crazy,' I muttered, 'what can be doing this?'

'This whole damned place gets ever crazier,' breathed Bernard, placing an arm against the wall to steady himself.

We tried again to move on but still could not, then Melina, her eyes closed, stretched her right arm slowly out beyond the invisible barrier and said, 'Wait, I think I – I feel it begins to probe my thoughts.'

166

'It what?' I asked. 'You mean it understands you?'

'Is something speaking to you?' asked Sunita in a low voice.

'No, not speaking - not words. It is as if comprehension flows to and from me, as if I know without having learned and because of this it tries to understand what I, what *we* are. There is no malice, there is no emotion. There is only curiosity - a deep curiosity because we are unknown life-forms.'

'But Melina,' Karin asked, 'what *is* it?'

'That it exists is the only answer I can give to you at this moment.' She opened her eyes and turned to us. 'If we are to know more then we must go further. This it will allow.' She stepped forward to confirm there was no longer any resistance, took cautious paces on then turned to enter the chamber from where the light spilled. I'll admit my hand was already slipping into my utility pocket when I followed her with Karin, Suita and Bernard close behind. Once there we stood and gazed in awed silence. What faced us a couple of metres before us in that small, chill, light-shimmering, domed white chamber made no sense at first. A transparent globe, less than half a metre across, rested some two metres from the floor upon a slender white pedestal. Within the globe a myriad points of blue light swirled about in seemingly random directions, clustering, dissipating, slowing then speeding suddenly. I tried to move closer, intending to walk around the thing, but I found I could not. Again that invisible barrier. For a time none of us spoke. We stared at the globe and I for one, standing next to Melina, found it almost hypnotic. I heard Melina say under her breath, 'It surveys, it oversees all that lies within this domain. It knew we were coming. It watched us and now it is entering deeper into my mind. It is aware of what has happened and through my thoughts it has discovered why it happened, though only now is it beginning to comprehend what we truly are and why we are here.'

That the thing must possess considerable power I was beginning to appreciate. The sensation I felt in Orion's force field during acceleration was evident for some moments but here it was more profound, as if every cell in my body was charged by – by I don't know what. And for some brief but anxious moments I was unable to move until able to look at the others and read their responses. They obviously had shared my experience. Karin clutched my arm and Bernard muttered, 'The damned thing is able to freeze us; I don't like that.'

Catching her breath and flexing the fingers of her part raised hands, Sunita asked Melina, 'This is a totally artificial life form you are talking to is it not?'

Melina relaxed her gaze upon the globe then turned slowly to answer, 'On Earth they once called it artificial intelligence but this must be of an order equal at very least to anything developed by humans even today. It has maintained control throughout this realm for countless ages, its power drawn from deep beneath the planet. Those who created it did so when they knew their world was to die. They did this to protect and preserve their kind here beneath the surface and it is a domain larger by far than we have been able to see.'

'Then as we already guessed,' I said, 'Xenonia must have been a world of divided interests even more than Earth once was, with some cultures highly advanced and others far less so.'

'That is as you say,' she replied, 'with much greater disparity here on Xenonia.'

'So whatever they were, the ones who created it,' I asked, 'where are they now? Are they far from here?' The answer, though, was already stirring in my mind.

Eyes once more closed, Melina's attention was fixed again upon the globe as she replied, 'Brett, this is difficult for me but I - I see now - they - they are long ago gone.'

'Gone where?' Karin asked. 'And why?'

The light particles within the globe were moving more rapidly, forming spirals that rotated, changing from light to dark then back again before dissipating into small, swirling clouds.

Melina was silent for a time then answered, 'It is becoming clearer now. They were destroyed through their own weaknesses. Intellectual and cultural progress was no longer possible in this domain below the surface. Only survival mattered so in time they descended into tribalism and conflict. There arose a desire among some to control the entity we stand before, which they had come to believe was a god dedicated to serve them, so that one group might find a way to direct its power against another. Yes, they had become a threat to their own ancestors' ultimate creation and so it eventually destroyed them.

'How did it – how did it do that?' Bernard asked guardedly.

Her answer was not calculated to instil us with confidence. 'The creature that would have attacked us – many more like it were created to eliminate the threat.'

'Sounds like a wholesale massacre,' put in Bernard.

'It is an entity set now upon preserving itself,' Melina continued, 'and all life here for no other reason than that. It can never evolve as do the creatures we encountered but justifies its existence through a memory that is almost infinite.'

'So if left alone,' said Karin, 'it'll go on as it now is for as long as Xenonia lasts, and that could be at least as long again as it's already existed – maybe longer.'

'That is so,' confirmed Melina.

'Then might it regard *us* as a threat?' Bernard asked.

'Maybe it will,' I muttered. 'I took out one of its pets a short while back.'

Melina paused and stared up at the globe as if to ask Bernard's very question. 'It is as yet undecided,' she answered.

'Are you saying it is confused?' Sunita asked.

'It is analysing,' she replied, 'because we are something it has never before encountered but so far it senses we have no ill intentions even though we killed one of its creatures.'

'But the one back there was set on killing us,' I said. 'How does that fit into the scheme of things around here now what we saw as an enemy is wiped out?'

Again she hesitated then replied, 'As you surmised, it was one of several top predators and so those remaining continue to help regulate the animal population. That creature regarded us as a threat to be eliminated but we defended ourselves as might be expected here or anywhere else in nature.'

'And can any of those things get up this far?' Bernard asked. I guess we all could understand his concern.

'No,' came her reply, 'nothing that lives out there can go beyond the outer edge of the area we at first crossed.'

'Most reassuring,' Bernard muttered, then Melina turned wide-eyed to say, 'I can no longer think properly. My mind is overwhelmed with images I do not understand except that - that some of those images are of us, of our very selves. It – it intends to create our likenesses to better understand what we are - I know it does.'

'We should get out while we can,' Bernard responded, 'in case the brain here takes a dislike to the real us. It stopped us from entering a while back by some sort of force field and had us seize up so there's no telling what else it could do.'

'Yes,' agreed Sunita, 'we must not outstay our welcome.'

'I don't recall we ever had a welcome,' I responded.

We began to back slowly away, all the time gazing at the light-dancing entity until we rounded the corner to the shorter passage. We reached the main passage, the way out, and from there observed our three spiders at the far entrance. As we approached, Cleo raised up on her eight legs for attention and with her antennae quivering urgently she announced, 'Brett, the microbots you had me send; they returned to say Tony has suffered damage and is no longer able to communicate!'

'We tried to reach you,' said Freddy, 'but there was an unseen barrier we could not pass.'

'She's saying the micros are unable to communicate with Tony,' I informed the others.

'What the hell could have happened up there?' asked Bernard.

I had my suspicions when I asked Ginger, 'Do you know where Franz Bergmann is?'

'He returned only two minutes ago and re-entered where you had earlier been,' she answered.

'So it seems he's in there looking for us,' I said. 'I wonder why.'

'Perhaps he's feeling lonely,' quipped Bernard.

'There is once more danger,' said Melina and we hesitated.

'What danger - where?' I asked. We looked about but couldn't see any threat.

'I am still confused,' she answered, 'but it is not far away.'

We retraced our steps to the green edge and stayed put while I called out by open sound as well as by radio, 'Bergmann, where are you? Bergmann, we're leaving and going back to the ground vehicle!'

For eternal seconds we peered about but there was no response, then Karin said, 'We don't need to wait around do we, Brett. He cleared off without a word and has his own transport waiting up there.'

'Okay let's ...' I began, then a bush was shoved aside some twelve or so metres to our left and Franz Bergmann stepped out. The gun he held was pointed at us. He remained where he was with a smile broadening the face behind his visor. 'Franz,' I called, 'what're you playing at?'

'So here you are!' he responded. 'I was looking in the wrong place but no matter.'

'Franz, lower that gun!' demanded Bernard. 'What's the meaning of this?'

I was reaching into my pocket, casually as I could, and had already slipped fingers about my own pistol when Bergmann replied, 'You, Commander, and those with you have conspired against me. I was meant to head this project from the very beginning but you determined I should have no part in it. But now I will do as I must and I will return to Earth alone.'

Melina had switched her radio to cut Bergmann out and said, 'Brett, his thoughts are very strong. The man is quite irrational and he thinks to kill us all.' Her voice was oddly calm.

She had no need to tell me what was on his twisted mind. We had to keep him talking and hope he might relax. I said to Sunita, who was standing right by me, 'See if you can reason with him. Tell him he can get home well before us and take whatever credit he wants.'

'Franz,' she called, 'what if I come with you as you have all along wished! Brett will agree with your returning first and I will support whatever claims you make.'

I wished she hadn't offered to go with him as she'd have been in the same danger as he was from Orion's response unless I could put a stop to it.

'You should have thought of that earlier, Sunita,' he responded. 'Such a pity, and you, all of you, know that now is impossible. The records, you see, would go against me with you as living proof whatever you said. Yes, I must return alone.'

'Bergmann,' I called, gripping my gun, 'Orion will prevent your leaving no matter what you do down here.'

'You kindly informed me of that possibility a while back, Commander. I will return to Earth in the service vessel, in cryosleep perhaps, but first I will have the shuttle connect with Orion. She carries explosives I had designated for possible use here and these I will detonate to destroy your precious vessel together with the cargo ship you allowed to accompany her.'

'You've worked most of this out well in advance, haven't you, Franz,' I said, easing my gun slowly upwards as far as I dared without him spotting it. I knew I could bring him down with a single shot but he'd have a split second chance to fire first and might hit one of us. It would possibly be fatal if we couldn't get back to Orion quickly enough.

'I did not waste the time I spent alone,' he responded.

Through my mind ran the possibility of having our three bots go for him then drawing my gun in what I hoped would be the resulting confusion. But when he stretched out his arm to raise his gun higher, pointing directly at me, and said, 'I think now I must leave,' I knew there was no time for anything more and yelled to the others, 'Get aside!' I crouched with my own gun drawn, my finger squeezing the trigger, but I did not fire because of what happened next. In those raging moments I saw the bushes open behind him. Something, a sound maybe, had alerted, had distracted him. Bergmann spun about - but too late! The thing leapt at him, another of those horrific creatures that had threatened us by the well. Bergmann screamed and fired into the air. Amidst gunshot echoes the creature snarled aloud, fastening hard about him in an intimate embrace of death, its teeth sinking deep into his shoulder, one of its clawed lower limbs ripping through his protective suit to penetrate deep into his innards. Both fell to the ground and despite its lesser size the thing was trying to drag him back, kicking, screaming and venting blood. I darted forward, halted two strides away, aimed, put a bullet of mercy into Bergmann's heart then another into the head of the creature that suddenly had switched its attention to me. I watched it collapse, into the undergrowth, still holding hard onto its dead victim. Aware of the turmoil that had arisen from within the bushes I stepped back to where my companions remained set in fearful disbelief, Karin with hands pressed ether side of her helmet, Sunita and Bernard clutching one another and wide-eyed Melina with a hand instinctively raised to the lower area of her visor.

We stood a while in silence, looking from one to the other. At last I said, 'We could never have saved him.'

'Do we try to retrieve his body?' Karin asked when we'd all had time to think more clearly. I don't believe she expected an affirmative.

'You mean once we can detach that thing still holding onto him,' I replied. 'No, whatever else lives in there will soon make a meal of both and anyway we have no means of containing or carrying his remains.'

'Let's be thankful for that,' muttered Bernard.

There were scurrying sounds from amidst the bushes close to where Bergmann and the killer beast had fallen as the odd lizard-like or crab-like creature made a fleeting appearance on its way with unseen others to a generous feast while still more circled or hovered in the air above. I briefly considered retrieving his gun and just as quickly decided not to. It could stay as a memento of our visit as had Melina's earrings at the last place.

'That bastard would have seen us all left down on this damned planet as corpses,' declared Bernard. 'Let's get to the surface before that thing in the bubble decides we're its enemy. We don't know what it's capable of.'

'I'm sure some of us do,' I muttered, glancing at Melina. Capable of just about anything around there was my guess.

'I sense its renewed attention upon us,' said Melina. 'We ought not to remain here.'

We didn't need a show of hands for that so with our bots ambling ahead we reached the passage leading to the chamber where the Entity, the being, the super-brain or whatever you'd care to call it was perched on top of its post and had unknowingly earned its title as a pronoun. Further along where the main passage began to ascend, we halted to take a backwards look across that incredible scene of alien life forms reaching away beneath the clustered lights of the cavern roof.

'There must be a whole area of interconnected chambers and voids,' said Bernard, 'all of them teeming with life. And that sea, or a part of it, could be accessed by much of it.'

'Brett,' said Karin, 'the deserted place we visited - it was suggested at the time we let the bots explore it further; we could do that here could we not.'

'I guess we could; we have another few days and who knows what else will turn up. There may be larger forms of life further inside.'

'Something bigger maybe than that thing you shot,' added Bernard.

'Bergmann's genes and the microorganisms he carried,' said Sunita, 'are now released into this environment. It will unfortunately be contaminated.'

'That's true,' Karin agreed, 'and we can only guess what the long term effects might be unless…'

She was cut short when Melina startled us with a cry of, 'Oh, look – look there!' She pointed with quivering arm outstretched towards the nearest line of bushes; a spot some four or so metres from where Bergmann had died.

We stared hard. We were dismayed at what we were seeing. There were five figures – human figures, stepping slowly out onto the green area which they crossed until halting at the edge where they grouped together. I was held fascinated yet alarmed as I knew must be my companions. I adjusted my visor to zoom in and in awed silence they did the same. Except for Melina. The figures we looked upon were without doubt meant to be images of ourselves they were ghostly pale and it was difficult to make out what each was wearing until Karen exclaimed, 'It's like our ordinary off-duty clothes they have on – that's how far the thing has plumbed our minds!'

'So it's even looked into our past,' said Bernard.

The one that appeared to emulate Karin raised an arm toward us as did the equally bizarre likeness of myself. They were not well defined, as I said, except for their eyes which now magnified were unnervingly large and sharp with their sinister gaze concentrated intensely upon us.

'They are gesturing for us to join them,' declared Melina. 'They appear as ourselves but I sense there is little conscious thought. I believe the Entity wants us to return to where it will set aside those figures it has created and take control of us. I feel this strongly though it is attempting to confuse me and will soon succeed. We presently stand beyond the full power of the Entity but I assure you we may soon be in great danger.'

In spite of what she'd said, fascination had taken control of us; yes, a compelling fascination. We were staring back at those eyes; hypnotising eyes that merged as one to fill our vision, to peer into us and demand we banish all fears and concerns from our minds. I for one began to feel that time and our present situation were no longer of any consequence. I and the other three were about to step forwards when Melina's voice rang through the haze. 'Brett!' It echoed as a gong within my head. I – we, snapped out of our collective trance. I switched to regular vision and had the others do likewise as cold reality once again stared us in the face. The figures created by the Entity were stepping forward as if to meet us. 'Okay' I declared, 'let's get out of here!' I didn't relish the idea of meeting up with a second hand copy of myself.

'It felt like they or something was taking me over,' I heard Bernard mutter as Sunita, eyes closed for the moment, took a hold of his arm. 'I hope they cannot follow us,' she breathed.

'I doubt they will,' responded Karin, 'the cold and lack of oxygen wouldn't allow it.'

'Brett,' informed Melina as we took a few steps on, 'we have passed the limit of the Entity's power; its creators never intended it to reach beyond where the life it presides over could go. We are free of it but can never return for it will surely destroy us and our robots if we do.'

We needed no convincing but regardless of our pressing desire to leave we felt compelled to take a final lingering look at those now motionless, still staring images of humanity before we continued the uphill trek out of that astonishing and potentially fatal subterranean realm. And there was Tony - we had to find out why our spiderbot was unable to communicate. Orion would be wondering why also and she might send misleading messages to Mars and Earth. We had much to think about on the way, apart from the appalling death of Franz Bergmann. We pondered over what might become of those likenesses of ourselves. Melina and Sunita were convinced the Entity could have created them in more complete form if given greater opportunity. They would breathe the air as we ourselves could have done had we taken the risk but they surely would not have gained our minds and our memories. Or I hoped they wouldn't. And should they possess the will to survive I fancied they might end up as some sort of grim experiment to see how long our physical kind would last within the ecosystem given what we'd already witnessed. One thing I was sure about – Melina, in calling my name, had quite possibly saved our lives. She had opened her mind to its limit and the Entity, on coming to realise fully what we were, had too late made its last throw.

Bernard sidelined my thoughts when he said, 'Brett, it may happen some time to Earth; a passing star really could disrupt our own system and bring about what has happened here.'

'Life on Mars might survive as it is a good while longer,' I offered. 'After all, our communities are self-sustaining and we'd continue to generate our own light and heat for the biodomes.'

'But what kind of existence would that be,' responded Sunita, 'with a world very much colder than Mars already is, without a sun to illuminate even the deserts and contact and trade with Earth eventually gone.'

'Quite so,' added Bernard, 'and in the end humanity might lose the will to continue. Might even end up with something like we met with here.'

'Well that's not about to happen,' informed Karin. 'We'd most likely know centuries in advance if another sun was heading our way, though what we'd do about it is another matter.'

These were subjects that would feature in many conversations to come. What our robots would have done had we succumbed here had not been foremost in my thoughts. Then I was thinking, a shot or two of Orion's bourbon wouldn't go amiss.

Eventually, with the temperature below minus one-ninety we saw stars ahead of us framed by the opening. Minutes later we emerged from beneath the overhang to find our fourth bot lifeless on the frozen ground. With our lights on him I noted the bullet holes. I stepped out and called Orion to say we were returned to the surface; the Apollo lights flooded on and back came the message, 'Brett, I was unable to contact you via Tony. Your relays were terminated by a method I was unable to ascertain. There is also a message from Mars awaiting your attention.'

'Okay Orion, we'll head for the ground vehicle and send up all our information on the way back to our pick-up point.' Turning my attention to the inert bot I asked Cleo, 'Is there any life left in Tony?

Cleo stepped to her motionless companion, her antennae quivering, and began to tap-tap-tap with her forelegs over various parts of his body. 'There is much internal damage,' she said, 'but the memory is intact and I am able to read it. I am conversing with Orion also and she says this unit will be repairable once returned.'

Bernard and I carried the stricken bot between us with Karin, Sunita, Melina and the three other spiders following. What a strange sight we would have presented had there been anyone to watch; tramping a few metres across that utterly desolate place in an alien pool of light. Once aboard the GV we proceeded beneath the Apollos to our starting point, above which Orion, having left the cargo vessel in orbit, hovered in readiness to pick us up. On the way there Orion confirmed she would have two of the bots deal with Tony, to reproduce and replace those parts that were damaged. We were not disposed to accepting the message from Joe and Amalia, until back onboard Orion, through the sterilisation procedure and divested of our environmental suits.

A while later we were on the control deck, each relaxing with welcome hot coffee, served by Cleo, when the main display lit up to reveal Joe seated in his office together with Amalia.

'Hi everyone!' greeted Amalia with hand raised.

'Hi!' repeated Joe. 'All is well here so we hope all is well out there and Orion is looking after you. Not too much going on in that last place you visited was there; sad but pretty interesting all the same. I wonder what they, whoever or whatever it was carved out all those passages and rooms looked like; one hell of a job that must have been. From the last report you sent, that third area looked more promising so maybe like the first there will be enough going on there to keep you happily occupied. And that fool, Bergmann - he might be locked away on his own with nothing to do other than keep himself looking tidy but there's trouble waiting for him big time when he returns to Earth and he has to be well aware of that by now. There's been little comment so far from the powers back there. They're waiting for a more comprehensive report and the goddamned media are jumping out of their socks for information. They've already created their own fantasy world on your behalf so they'll need putting right.'

'Then the fantasy world we just left behind shouldn't disappoint them,' I muttered.

'And Karin,' said Amalia, 'your team at the space station observatory wish me to inform you that Xenonia is already moving out from the Kuiper belt. This is a little sooner than predicted although it is slow enough not to affect your ongoing plans.'

'Okay,' concluded Joe, 'we'll sign off now but we'll look forward to your next message that I'm sure will be with us in due course.'

'Yes, we look forward to knowing all about whatever next you may have discovered,' smiled Amalia. 'Take care now.'

The images faded, the stars beyond reappeared and we finished our coffees. There was something else that next had to be dealt with - Bergmann's ship. Were we to leave it there? 'Orion!' I called, 'the shuttle used by Franz Bergmann is still on Xenonia's surface; are you able to recover this and bring it up into orbit?'

Not a half minute passed before the answer came, 'I have scanned the shuttle and its contents and I find access to its controls remain denied. Should I attempt such access then the vessel will explode with considerable violence.'

'It's true, isn't it,' remarked Karin, 'Bergmann did plan his actions some way back, as you said.'

'So, what if anything might we do with the shuttle apart from letting it stay down there?' asked Bernard.

I thought for a moment then said, 'Okay – right.'

'Brett,' Karin said, 'I think I know what you're planning – something we touched on earlier.'

'Yes, that's it. You may recall Bergmann saying his shuttle carried four helibots and that each of these contained a number of micros, presumably like our own flying bots; well I've figured out a use for them. Orion,' I asked, 'how stable are the explosives that vessel contains and can we somehow get inside it to recover the main contents? Can we get the helibots out of there without blowing the whole thing sky high?'

A modest pause then, 'I find the explosives will remain stable provided we do not attempt to activate the vessel's hyperdrive. Two of our spiderbots can be equipped to cut away one side of the shuttle. Should they succeed I will attempt contact with the helibots and have them move safely away.'

Orion had given me the answers I wanted. 'Then,' I ordered, 'have Freddy and Ginger go down there in the cargo ship then take one of the skimmers to the surface so they can see to getting the helibots out. Have the helibots move well away from Bergmann's shuttle and stay where they are then get the cargo ship back up here with our bots.'

'Yes, I do know what you're up to,' smiled Karin, and the look on Melina's face told me she herself certainly did.

'Then maybe you'll fill *me* in,' said Bernard.

'Yes, me too,' smiled Sunita. 'This sounds most interesting.'

'Okay, if we're successful I'll have Orion transfer all our survey information about Xenonia down to Bergmann's helibots. They can then continue exploration on our behalf and use their micros for in-depth searches at new locations. At each stage they'll relay their findings to us and so on to Mars.'

'Are you saying we're soon to quit?' asked Bernard. 'Brett, I thought you always favoured humans being fully involved with this project.'

'So I did and so we have but I reckon we've justified our presence by now, provided we all agree.'

'This abandoned world does not want us,' said Melina. 'The Entity we encountered would have destroyed us had we remained much longer within its reach.'

'To continue as we are,' said Karin, 'would involve us in much more time and Orion's surveys, extensive as they've been these last few days, have revealed nothing of equal promise to compare with where we've so far managed to gain access.'

The others agreed that letting the helibots take over was a logical plan. No one would have any regrets over our leaving Xenonia and I was convinced we'd made our grand gesture in pursuing matters as far as we had. We took ourselves to our quarters then returned a half hour later to order more coffee, and sit before the main display. There we watched from synchronous orbit as Freddy and Ginger, aided by a cluster of Apollo lights, and having become experts with plasma cutters, remove a section from one side of the shuttle. Under the control of Orion the helibots clambered out then, rotor blades spinning and lights shining they drifted over to the side of the amphitheatre close to where we had parked the ground vehicle when down there earlier. Our bots returned to the skimmer that now transferred back to the cargo ship where the Apollo lights were already called in. We watched with, in my case at least, considerable satisfaction as Bergmann's shuttle exploded violently into a spreading shower of brightly glowing embers. There could be no fire, of course, not in the largely oxygen-free atmosphere. With our bots back on board Orion, the cargo ship was returned to the surface where she would be left in the amphitheatre, serving as a base from which to recharge the helibots and via these, the micros. The cargo ship's power would remain available for many years – Earth years, that is, rather than Mars years, and she would cover much of Xenonia as the planet drifted on her way into deepest space with the stars as her companions. Even then we hoped there would still be much to learn with feedback from our abandoned assets. And there were still, of course, the latest specimens from that last excursion for Sunita to examine.

Shortly after, Orion coupled up with the service ship so that our two vessels, now a consolidated unit, were ready to quit Xenonia. Before doing so, before our leaving orbit, I took myself into the service ship to see what, if anything Bergmann had left behind. In the small accommodation area were various items of his clothing, all precisely arranged, awaiting his return with nothing whatsoever out of place. Most obvious when I checked out the suit storage compartment was the briefcase laying open where he'd left it, awaiting the return of his pistol. Apart from a number of neatly arrayed personal items, there was a small box containing spare ammunition for the pistol. I left the case and their contents where they were.

'I doubt our Planet X will see more visitors for a very, very long time,' remarked Karin when I'd returned.

'Quite possibly never again,' added Bernard.

'But if others did go there,' I said, 'I wonder what they'd think on seeing what we'd left behind on the surface.'

'And what if they came upon my earrings?' Melina smiled.

'Utter confusion I imagine,' said Karin. 'But Xenonia may continue drifting in darkness as it has for countless millions more years with no further visits.'

'And when heat from her core gives out as it eventually must,' said Bernard, 'all life there will be ended. She'll be but a dead rock awaiting the end of the universe.'

With our next meal, our dinner, we enjoyed an excellent Cabernet Sauvignon produced by Orion to celebrate our leaving orbit. We now were but a sliver of warmth and life adrift within an indifferent, an unfathomable void. We talked further over what we'd seen and done until Orion prompted us to take our rest period.

In our quarters and readying for bed, I said to Karin, 'All we witnessed on Xenonia – I see no meaning behind any of it; no purpose other than a will to survive.'

'No, Brett, no meaning, no purpose. None whatsoever. And we might as well apply this to the whole of humanity. You'll recall what Melina said when we were down on that second visit and she reminded us there has to be an end to everything.'

'Yes, I recall that and I agree, though there are still people on Earth who think otherwise as we well know.'

'You mean those who still believe in something like the Entity,' she said.

'Sure, something like the Entity, but not something you can drop by to take a close look at. Anyhow, I don't see our existence coming to an end for some time yet but I reckon we've only one lifetime to make the best of what we have.'

'We most certainly do, dear,' she smiled, running her fingers softly down my cheek.

A little later I asked Karin if she fancied sharing a dream and she answered, 'Yes, Brett, I do. I know we're on our way home but we can pre-empt that in our sleep can't we and go again to some place warm and definitely sunny.'

I needed no convincing.

Sunlight

Before we headed for breakfast the following Orion day she confirmed to us that the helibots on

Xenonia were fully active but as we expected, nothing of any consequence had so far been detected. Karin brought up the subject of Bernard and Sunita. 'What will happen when we reach Mars?' she asked. 'We don't want to lose Sunita do we but Bernard will return to Earth.'

By then we were a third of the way on our journey back to Mars; the red planet being but a short way further from us in her orbit than when we left with Earth slightly closer and the Sun still a bright star amidst many others.

'I doubt Bernard and Sunita will want to part,' I replied, 'but I guess that's something only they can resolve. Presumably Melina will return to Earth. Doesn't say much, does she.'

'I'll ask her later what she hopes to do,' said Karin.

Neither of her questions were to be addressed over breakfast because Orion had already informed us there was another message downloading from Mars and we speculated over what the reaction might be to our third descent. Little else was said over the table although Bernard and Sunita had passed several smiling glances at each other. Soon enough the five of us were ready to go to the control deck. Once seated before the main display I gave Orion the go-ahead to download. Joe van Allen, for once since we'd left Mars, appeared somewhat anxious, as did Amalia Barbosa sitting close by him.

'What a hell of a time you had down there!' he declared as Amalia nodded in sympathy. 'And that goddamned, whatever you want to call it, that went for you and the other that did for Franz Bergmann. Good you were armed though I had no idea you were taking your old gun. Well what you came across has everyone talking here and on Earth; it's big, big news and I guess they'll be clamouring for interviews as soon as you return.'

'We'll be glad to have the five you safely home,' put in Amalia. 'Meanwhile, Karin's team at the observatory will be receiving whatever information your bots send over from Xenonia in the hope they find something more of interest. This could, and we hope will, go on for many years.'

As she spoke I imagined the cargo vessel, the helibots and their flying micros going about their lonely business, abandoned on that world of sunless desolation.

'Look,' said Joe, 'it's evening here so by the beginning of our tomorrow, you'll be most of the way home. One hell of a party is what we're planning in the biodome so be ready to have yourselves spoiled! That's it for now.'

We sat around talking for the first half of the break period and picking up some of the news from Earth about ourselves to find much of it had been subject to an amusing degree of speculation. It was after we got together over lunch that Bernard and Sunita revealed their thoughts on the subject Karin and I had raised between ourselves before breakfast.

'When we reach Mars,' said Sunita, 'Bernie and I will need to sort things out between ourselves.'

It was the first time I'd heard her address him in such a familiar manner in spite of their closeness.

'I will be returning to Earth on the service vessel because of existing commitments,' informed Bernard, 'but before that I hope to sound out Joe van Allen regarding a possible position on Mars.'

'You should do exactly that,' responded Karin. 'It worked for me a while back as it did more recently for Sunita.'

'It certainly did,' agreed Sunita. 'I find the research work I undertake on Mars allows me greater responsibility and is more readily appreciated than it was on Earth.'

'I think you might find Joe sympathetic,' I added. 'And there may be other things you can give a hand to as I know from my own experiences.'

Karin turned to Melina and asked, 'And you, dear, have you anything in mind or will you return to Europe?'

'I will return because I was involved in a group project that has almost another year to run. After that I will be free to consider my future.'

'Well perhaps you will consider us as a part of your future when you do,' smiled Sunita.

My thoughts had gravitated back to Joe's plans for the space museum on Mars and I had a few ideas of my own to go over with him. Yes, a good few ideas and although there was much work ahead this project should be relatively problem free. I was sure Karin would find time to become involved as well. After that brief discussion I had Orion open up the view ahead and there was a most welcome sight.

Our star was not yet as large as when seen from Mars but soon enough we would commence deceleration prior to entering Mars orbit where we'd find the red planet bathed in glorious sunlight.

Author's Afterword

My thanks to Lynda Buxton for her welcome assistancein reading through and pointing out the numerous texturaland other deficiencies in my work.

More books by the author

THE MAN WHO SOUGHT ETERNITY
SHADOW OF THE BEAST
RETURN OF THE HERO
THE SINGING STONES
THE DEVIL IN EDEN
TITAN
I MEDEA
ELECTRA HIDDEN WORLDS Volumes 1 and 2

www.jeffreypeterclarke.com